STICKS & STONES

D0996237

GLENNA THOMPSON

outskirtspress

DENVER, COLORADO

Outskirts Press, Inc.
http://www.outskirtspress.com

PB ISBN: 978-1-4787-1961-8
HB ISBN: 978-1-4787-1949-6

Outskirts Press and the "OP" logo are trademarks belonging to Outskirts Press, Inc.

PRINTED IN THE UNITED STATES OF AMERICA

Chapter One

ABBY WARREN DISCONNECTED the phone call and haphazardly fired the cordless receiver toward her red velour couch in frustration. It missed its intended mark, torpedoing past and crashing into a heavy leg of the black wrought-iron table behind it, smacking end over end across the scarred walnut flooring before coming to rest on top of the steel floor grate between the kitchen and dining room-turned-art studio of her tiny apartment. The commotion caused two distinct reactions—the first was a startled yowl from Brewtus, an oversized snobbish orange tabby temporarily residing with her; and second, an obnoxious staccato of whacks to her floor which came from the apartment below.

Mrs. Davis, an elderly widow who at moments like this seemed quite spry for her age, was pounding her discontent on her ceiling with a broomstick handle, again. With an animated grunt, Abby shoved her long, dark chestnut hair away from her face, rolled her jade green eyes and looked toward Brewtus who was now elegantly, for lack of a better description, perched on her lone kitchen countertop with his hind leg stuck straight up in the air while he concentrated solely on grooming himself. He was a pretentious creature and she was now fuming that she'd agreed to take him in for the duration of her neighbor's business trip to Spokane. While Nicholas

Pratt was off taking photos of the picturesque mountain terrain, his beer drinking roommate, hence the name Brewtus, had taken over her living space as if he owned it himself.

Childish as it was she stomped the thick rubber heel of her work boot on the floor in irritation. She really didn't give a damn if she'd interrupted a stimulating episode of Jeopardy in the apartment below. Her world had just blown up. Her father had been injured in an accident and her mother expected her to drop everything and come home to help out. It hadn't mattered that Abby was dealing with some rather large issues of her own at the moment. It's not that she didn't care. However, she was smack in the middle of a possible expansion for her glassware company. On top of that, she was hastily scouring the city for a new apartment as the cost of her lease was about to skyrocket. She had only five weeks left to find something suitable for her move.

Abby felt an unexpected stab of guilt. St. Louis was only a six-hour drive from her hometown of Mills Pond, Kansas. Still, she didn't have the time or energy it would take to go home, even for a few days. Swearing none to quietly, she clomped over to the couch, picked up a black decorative pillow—at least it had been black before Brewtus infiltrated her humble abode—and tossed the fur infested cushion onto the floor. Disheartened, she plunged her five-foot-seven frame onto the couch seat causing a dull thud when she landed. Forcing her back into the cushion, she heaved a heavy sigh. She'd known this day would eventually come. It was inevitable. She'd left Mills Pond ten years ago, vowing never to return. Ugly things from the past awaited her there and the last thing she wanted to do was face them.

With a neat stack of plywood snuggly wedged beneath one arm, Chad Austin thrust open one side of the double glass door with his jean-covered hip, kicked it wider with the toe of his boot and walked out of the store. He was tall, over six-foot, with thick mahogany hair and sable brown eyes that he'd often heard compared to the color of pecans. His body was trim and fit through the middle extremities while his upper torso widened appropriately. Thick ropes of muscle spiraled beneath the tanned skin of his arms and neck, clearly visible beyond the pale gray T-shirt he wore. He was built like a football player, well, at least he had been.

High School ball had led to college and somehow career day with the NFL snuck up and passed him by. Not that it bothered him much. He'd managed to build a successful construction company in Tulsa at a wet-behind-the-ears age of twenty-four. After the death of his father two years ago, he'd sold it and moved back to Mills Pond to be closer to his family. At age twenty-nine, he had money in the bank and owned twenty acres of land outside of town on which he'd built a two-story log cabin. With some surprise, the structure had brought a good deal of enthusiasm from the locals.

But the fact that he'd gained a solid community reputation wasn't the reason for the ridiculous smile plastered across his features as he carefully carried his haul to the truck. His trip to Warren Lumber had bore him much more than product. He felt giddy, though he knew that was not a word likely to be associated with a masculine trait. It was however, the only word that would correlate precisely with his current emotional state. His entire body was abuzz with anticipation. Abby Warren, daughter of Paul and Joyce Warren, was coming home.

Abby, with her slender, lithe frame, dark brown hair and distinctive green eyes was headed back to Mills Pond. His heartbeat quickened. He felt like an adolescent trapped in a man's body.

He'd had such a tremendous crush on her in high school. That he was a year older and had been part of the popular crowd—as much of a crowd a school of less than three hundred students could generate—while she'd been shy and reclusive had made no difference to him. His brother Chase had been in the same class as Abby and had dated her best friend, Holly Miles. It was through that triangle of friendship that he had gotten to know her.

His dating preference had been the cheerleader types, those bold and attractive girls who were inevitably paired with the school jocks since the beginning of time. By his senior year he'd grown bored with them, searching out instead, the intense focus and infinite intrigue that Abby brought to his senses. She'd been witty and artistic. He'd had to be quick on his feet to keep up with her. Her solid green gaze had pierced his chest and he'd found himself time and time again, lost in the vast pools of Caribbean splendor her eyes offered. It had been enough to drive him mad. Mad for her and angry with himself because he'd never worked up the courage to tell her how he felt. Fear, plain and simple, had kept him silent. He was terrified that she'd reject him so he'd never given her the chance.

He'd been shallow and stupid and more than just a little dramatic. Of course, he'd loved drama club in those days and the plays he'd performed in put flighty perceptions into his youthful mind. He chuckled to himself remembering the severe wavering that had raged between body parts. It had been a constant battle tamping down hormones on the rampage. He hoped ten years had improved his maturity level. At least he'd lived through a couple of broken hearts since then and learned that he could survive.

After his return to Mills Pond he had inquired about Abby and discovered that she was an artist, a glassblower to be more specific, which didn't surprise him. He'd wasted many an afternoon in the art room watching her work. She was single and living in

St. Louis. Now that he knew she was coming home, he was going to make up for lost time. His stupid adolescent fears were going to be chalked up to past failures. He would not squander the opportunity a second time. In fact, he planned to pounce on her with his complete arsenal blazing. Well, maybe not all at once, but he would leave her with no doubts as to where he stood. No fear this time around, only sheer determination.

With his free hand, he dropped the tailgate and carefully slid the plywood into the bed of his truck. Whistling to himself, he slammed it back into place and fought to keep his feet from floating off the ground as he made his way to the cab. He felt dizzy as he opened the door and climbed into the driver's seat. Pulling the door closed, he looked in the mirror at the warehouse behind him and smiled again knowing that the next time he visited, she would be there.

—⁌((◐))⁍—

Rumor had it Abigail Warren was returning to Mills Pond. Paul Warren, her father, had been hit by a speeding semi-truck on the highway during a routine delivery and flown by helicopter to the hospital. He was in pretty bad shape, from what he'd heard. Bad enough to bring Abby home after a decade long hiatus. His heart pumped a little harder in his chest and he slapped the steering wheel with the palm of his hand hard enough that it left a stinging sensation behind. After all this time, would she be able to stir up the past?

He'd had a problematic youth and he'd made mistakes. There was one whopper in particular that he'd hidden from everyone. As far as he was concerned, he'd atoned for his sins. Besides, he had a family now and couldn't afford for the truth to come out. Abby

Warren was the only one who could pose a potential problem for him. He would need to keep an eye on her. If he felt even an inkling of a threat, he would force her out of town again. In fact, he was not above doing whatever it took to ensure the dark secret of his youth stayed buried.

Chapter Two

ABBY'S HANDS TIGHTENED on the steering wheel of her cherry red 1990 Acura Integra. Her dark hair whipped around her face as a hot arid wind gusted through the half-open windows. She abhorred Kansas in August. The grass and fields were burned brown from the summer-long beating they'd taken by the scorching sun and the ground was laced with cracks big enough to swallow her car whole. Rain was sadly needed and rarely gotten this time of year. With a leaded-ball of dread in the pit of her stomach, Abby headed southwest toward her childhood home of Mills Pond.

With each monotonous mile she logged on the lonely two-lane highway, her heart beat more rapidly within the deep confines of her tightly-wound chest. The thought of home no longer caused her to hyperventilate, though coming back may reverse that. Shortly after her high school graduation, tragedy struck and her closest friends and classmates had turned against her. At eighteen, she was young and naïve and had believed the best in people. The agony they had put her through had torn the only home she'd ever known out from beneath her. It got to the point that she was forced to leave town. That is, until now.

Two days ago she'd been fully focused on her life and her own set of problems. After her mother's ambush, she couldn't in good conscience abandon her family. She'd been gone a long time. Maybe things had changed. Maybe it was finally time to face the past and bury the hatchet, if at all possible. But as Mills Pond grew closer, the panic spreading through her veins turned the warm rushing river of her blood into an icy stream, trickling through her limbs. Brewtus must have sensed her unease. He nudged his way between the bucket seats and plopped his pudgy body into a big orange ball on the passenger seat. She met his blazing green eyes. The look he gave her was dismissive but the incensed yowl that crept from his throat was anything but.

"Sorry, buddy," she said, forcing her gaze back toward the highway in front of her. "It was either come along for the ride or face starving to death. Somehow I don't think Nick would appreciate the latter. As for me, I'm still on the fence."

Pushing away lingering thoughts of the mangy cat sitting beside her, she wondered briefly how many of her old classmates might still live there. Was she worrying prematurely? Mills Pond was a small town with a population bordering on just over three thousand souls. It was an impracticality that everyone she knew had remained. Abby prayed that Chase Austin had been one of those to move away—far, far away. He'd been the leader of the group that had bullied her into leaving home. Her shoulders tensed as a sharp stab of grief shot down her spinal cord. Holly Miles had been Abby's best friend since the first grade, though she'd also been Chase's girlfriend. The summer following their graduation had changed everything and she'd missed Holly's friendship terribly.

Abby drove by a green and white highway sign indicating her hometown was a mere seven miles away. A cold sweat broke across her skin. She hadn't suffered from acute anxiety attacks in over three years but she felt one coming on sure and fast. She had to get a grip. Her father was injured which left her parents lumberyard shorthanded. She was an only child and they needed her help. Time healed all wounds, right? Could it make them evaporate as well? Was it possible to waltz back into town and find acceptance? Deliberately applying reverse psychology to her wounded psyche, she could only hope it would be that simple.

It amazed her that the farm terrain had changed so little during the past decade. The acreage opened to fields dense with towering stalks of previously picked sweet-corn and maturing soybeans. Both looked as though the harsh sunlight was choking what bit of life still lingered. Once those fields were completely harvested, the remnants would be tilled back into the soil so that a crop of hard winter wheat could be planted after the first solid frost. Harvesting two crops with the same land enabled farmers to fully utilize their acreage. Among the fields, some newer, unfamiliar homes sat alongside older ones that she could distinctly recall.

Turtle Creek snaked alongside the roadway before swiftly banking to the left and disappearing entirely out of sight. More houses came into view—the Morrison's, the Beckman's, the Parker's—along with a large brick ranch sitting just off the highway to the right. This was definitely one of those newer homes. *The Bitterman's* was sprawled across the large motorhome shaped mailbox. It was a name she didn't recognize but she smiled as she passed the Crawford's place. The same old orange tractor, a 1961 Allis Chalmers if she could remember correctly, and wagon remained in place just beyond a deep drainage ditch in the huge front yard.

Abby knew she was only a mile out of town when she rolled past Deadwood Dick's bar. She shook her head and grinned. There was a story, or maybe more of a legend behind the name, but she'd never been in a position to learn what it was. She was utterly amazed that it was still standing. In fact, it looked pretty much the same as it had when she'd left. There was nothing fancy about it, just a big wooden-planked building painted an ugly, dull brown. The only identifier was a huge hand-carved sign that hung between two heavy wooden posts at the street entrance. From the numerous vehicles parked in front, it was obvious the old saloon continued to fuel a decent number of town folk.

A half-mile further on the right was a new antiques store and Karl's Gas & Tow. Abby had gone to school with Karl Dunkin and wondered briefly if he was the owner of the service station. Karl had graduated the year before Abby and hadn't been part of the group who had ruthlessly harassed her. She remembered that he was a big guy, stocky and muscular. He'd been interested in cars and football, not necessarily in that order. It was the high school football season that had put Mills Pond on the map. Everyone in town enjoyed the excitement of the big Friday night brawls. Talk about crowds-gone-wild! Abby suddenly missed those crazy days when hope of winning the state conference championship consumed the town.

She'd never been a popular girl, preferring instead to follow a more obscure route. Most of her spare time had been spent within the fumy confines of the art education suite. She'd played the saxophone as well, and was part of the marching band. She'd possessed her share of boy crushes, but had never been presented with an opportunity to act upon one. In fact, by the age of eighteen, she hadn't even experienced her first kiss. It was sad, but true. The town had taken that away from her too. Nearly missing her turn onto First Street, she shook herself out of her reverie. Gripping the wheel, she made a hasty left. Only sixteen short blocks to go and she would be in town square, the beating heart of Mills Pond.

Small, perfectly squared blocks of land dotted with older homes lined her path as she drove south. Most of these were familiar. The only new houses she'd spotted had popped up on the outskirts of town. The big old elm tree she'd spent many a summer climbing was still standing on the corner of First and Elm. Holly had fallen out of that tree when they were twelve and broken her arm. Because of her plaster cast, she'd been banned from the swimming pool and

Abby had spent that summer stuck inside with her watching Buffy the Vampire Slayer on HBO and dreaming about pop star or movie actor boyfriends while reading teen magazines and dancing to energetic tunes by Paula Abdul and New Kids on the Block.

Abby motored past the Spencer house, a huge three-story residence which had been transformed into a charming bed and breakfast. It was an older home with beautiful oak floors, crown molding, stained glass, and delicately painted accents. At one end of the wide front porch an old-fashioned wooden swing hung from the covered roof by polished silver chains. White wicker tables were strategically placed between four hunter green oversized wooden rockers, all of which created excellent curb appeal. The house was painted a crisp white with green trim, the same hue as the rockers and swing. Becky Spencer had been part of Chase Austin's group and Abby considered the fact that she might very well be involved with the alluring inn.

She realized she was close to downtown when she encountered the large, old maple trees lining each side of the street. They were beautiful in the fall as their leaves exploded with color, green bursting with different hues of yellow, orange and red. August summers could be unbearably hot but Kansas in October was breathtaking with its vibrant colors and cool, crisp air. The leaves would inevitably float to the ground covering the dormant yellowed grass in a thick carpet of dried crunchy brown carcasses. It was a sure sign the holidays were fast approaching and along with them, plummeting temperatures, ice and snow.

Abby braked for the stop sign at First and Main. She had reached downtown central. The middle square hosted a community park with a gazebo that stood in the center. Red brick streets bordered the square housing a host of small businesses including the bank, post office, library, city hall, Hancock Fabric's shop, Alcott Pharmacy, a doctor and dentist office in separate buildings, Hometown Movie Rentals, Macy's Café, Freddy's Ice Cream Parlor, The Gem movie theater, and the town hall recreation center. Abby could recall many gatherings here for picnics and celebrations. For a brief moment, the memory flooded her with regret. In her younger years, she'd run carelessly through the park with the mid-summer sun beating down upon her while she dreamed of marrying this boy or that one. At the time, she couldn't wait to bring her own family here to join in the town festivities. A lone tear trailed down her cheek as the vivid childhood dream melted away. Because of a lie, she'd been stripped of the joy those continued celebrations might have brought her. Because of a lie, her young life had been turned upside down. Because of a lie, she'd lost everything that had once been important to her.

A black Ford F150 Supercrew drew to a stop at the intersection of First and Main. It's Smittybitt billet grill and chrome side-step running bars gleamed brightly from the early afternoon sun. Though the truck was a major source of pride for him, he couldn't avoid the bright red Acura to his right that drew his attention. She was an older model that looked to be in excellent condition. It was definitely a nice little ride, right along with the long-haired brunette behind the wheel. She was undeniably a looker and a jolt of caution rushed through him. As the woman drove straight through the intersection, he decided to follow her. The red Acura maintained a straight course past Nash, Oak and Pine. The signal began to blink and she turned right onto Sycamore. It was the street he lived on. An odd mixture of excitement and dread coursed through him. The brunette continued on, passing both Second and Third Streets. The blinking light at the rear of her car began again and she turned into the third driveway on the left. The third driveway belonged to Paul and Joyce Warren. He felt as though he'd been punched in the gut and sucked in a deep breath. Abigail Warren had officially returned. Making a right turn at the intersection of Sycamore and Fourth Street, a half-block from his house, he headed in the direction of town square en route to the highway. As he drove away from her, he drew in a deep breath forcing his body to calm itself. There was nothing to do now but carefully watch and wait.

Chapter Three

ABBY'S FINGERS TREMBLED as she slowed the car to a stop and thrust the gearshift into park next to her father's blue Dodge Dakota and her mother's silver Chrysler Sebring. She closed her eyes and gulped in a deep breath, hoping the quick burst of stifling air would flush the nervousness from her system. It didn't. She opened her eyes. The house, which sat to her right, was a large two-story Victorian with a full wraparound porch. It was an old-fashioned house, a comfortable house. One she had loved growing up in.

"Welcome home, Brewtus," she said as her gaze slid away from her childhood home to the passenger seat where she was met with a peevish glare. The orange tabby quickly dismissed her, shifting focus instead to his immaculate grooming habits by licking his front paw a couple of times and dragging it over the top of his head. She wondered briefly how many baths cats in general took a day and how it compared to a human shower. She was stalling and she knew it.

With a heavy sigh she pushed the car door open and climbed out. Reaching her arms over her head, she stretched her stiffened muscles. The house was a slate gray color with crisp white trim instead of the pale yellow she remembered. The roof had been replaced as well, the black shingles swapped for those of a deep cornflower blue. The contrast between the house color and the white hanging baskets aligning the porch rafter filled with vivid orange and yellow Marigold puffs was striking. The three-car driveway consisted of a thick bed of loose gravel. The only weather protection offered was in the form of vastly sprawling limbs from the huge weeping willow she'd parked beneath. Her surroundings felt strange, yet familiar at the same time.

"Abigail!"

Abby turned to find her mother rushing down the back steps. She was wearing a yellow scoop-neck T-shirt, blue jeans, and brown work boots. *Jeans and boots in this heat, was she crazy?* Her mother's dark brown hair was cut short and stuck out at various angles around her head. The style was cute and made her look younger than her forty-nine years. Abby smiled, succumbing to the warm embrace offered as soon as she came within hugging distance.

Joyce Warren smiled brightly at her daughter. "It's so nice to have you home!"

Abby wasn't convinced yet, whether her homecoming was nice or not. There were too many uncertainties buried beneath the surface to be confident. Her mother's approval was one thing; the Mill's Pond community was something entirely different. "Thanks, Mom. How's Dad doing?"

"He's had two surgeries to repair his fractured leg. His left femur was shattered during the accident. Right now he's in a medically induced coma as a way to keep him completely still until some of the swelling has a chance to go down. The truck driver walked away without a scratch on him."

Abby dropped her arms and backed away. Drawing in another deep breath, she gave a stiff nod of her head. "I'm sorry," she said.

"They believe he'll make a full recovery. It's just going to take time and a lot of physical therapy," Joyce said. "That's why I need you here. I'm spending most of my time at the hospital and not enough at the lumberyard. The guys can handle the yard; it's the office where I need your help."

"Well, here I am," Abby said. She knew her voice didn't reflect the enthusiasm she wanted her mother to hear but she couldn't quite get past the tension she felt welling up inside.

"Can I help carry anything?"

"Thanks," Abby replied. "I only have a couple of bags. Oh, and a cat."

"A cat? I didn't think you liked cats."

"I don't," Abby said. "As a favor, I was cat-sitting for a neighbor who is out of town and on such short notice, couldn't find anyone willing to take him."

"Tell you what," Joyce said, "why don't I take your bag and you carry the cat?"

Abby felt the force of her mother's gaze as she bent through the window and pulled the keys from the ignition. Straightening, she walked to the back of the car, opened the lid and retrieved a medium-sized suitcase from her trunk. Slamming it closed, she handed the suitcase to her mother. "I'll follow you," she said.

The first step she took, her heel came down on a sharp rock that had made its way onto the upper-base of her flip-flop. Sucking in a deep breath in order to keep the curse spewing through her brain at bay, she shook the sandal, dislodging the hard jagged stone. *Welcome home*, she thought to herself as she opened the passenger door, grabbed the matching maroon tote bag off the floor and scooped up the pudgy yellow furball that wanted anything but and followed her mother up the back steps and into the kitchen.

As soon as the screen door banged shut behind her, Brewtus jumped from her arms and she was blindsided by the color yellow. Not a warm, sunny yellow. This was a deep, sunflower yellow that clung to the walls as if Big Bird had exploded. It was no wonder the cat had taken cover. When she blinked, the white cabinetry came into view, along with the blue and white checkered ceiling border and solid blue chair-rail that wrapped around the entire room. The cabinets, most with solid doors, a few with glass, the accompanying bar stools, and the table and chairs in the breakfast nook were all white. For contrast, the countertops were black marble while the refrigerator, stove, dishwasher, and microwave were made of stainless steel. All of it helped to diminish the dynamic hue of the yellow, softening it, but only slightly.

"Do you like it?" Joyce asked, her voice questioning while her facial expression remained one of wondrous awe as she gazed around the room. "Isn't it lovely?"

Abby nodded her head, a little in awe herself. "It's really something."

"Your dad thought I was crazy, but Chad did a beautiful job with the cabinets and the bar. You remember Chad Austin, don't you? You graduated together."

A quick tug of dread hit Abby like a fist to the stomach. She hadn't been here ten minutes and already she felt like an alien, a misfit, a loner standing on the outside looking in. She didn't belong here. As soon as her dad was on the mend, she would hit the road, pedal to the metal, and not look back. "Chad's a year older. I was in the same class with his brother, Chase."

Along with the stomach-punch, Abby felt a flutter like a kaleidoscope of butterflies taking flight. Chad Austin had been one of the few males in school to take even the slightest interest in her. Although only a year older, he seemed so much more mature than his brother. Abby remembered cheering from the stands at the football games. He'd been a wide-receiver for the Mills Pond Panthers. He was also in the honor society, loved acting in the school's theater productions, and in his spare time, managed to hang out in the art room with her. Well, not really *with* her, he just showed up at the same time she did. The way he'd looked her in the eye and offered honest critiques of her work had gained him a silent, steady admirer. She'd often pretended he would spend time in the art room because he liked her but she knew she was far from his type. The perky personality and pom-poms were definitely a missing factor. Still, it didn't negate those late night longings and thoughts of dreams that could never be.

"That's right. I'm sorry, Abby. I shouldn't have brought it up."

"It's okay. I'm not the same fragile girl that left here ten years ago. You don't have to walk on eggshells."

A sad smile crossed Joyce Warren's features. "I know this trip home wasn't easy for you."

Abby stood in the middle of the kitchen, the handle of her tote bag clasped tightly in her fist. She had no response, not even a clever little quip to put them both at ease. With eyes shimmering with the onslaught of tears, her mother moved toward her, slipping an arm around her shoulders in a way that suggested she was holding on tightly for fear her daughter would bolt as soon as she got the chance. She wasn't wrong in that assumption.

"Come on," she said softly as she began walking forward, dragging Abby with her toward the hallway that would lead to the rest of the house. "Your old bedroom is waiting for you."

While the kitchen color was bright and bold, the hallway was painted pale beige. Framed photographs hung on the wall to her right. Sadly, most were taken a decade or more ago. Abby's high school senior picture was adjacent to her framed graduation certificate. Beside it, a group picture of Abby and several classmates were posing in their caps and gowns after the ceremony. Abby stopped to gaze at the photo below it. She reached out an index finger to trace the rosy cheek of the girl frozen in the frame. In the photo, she and Holly stood arm in arm on the front porch, showing off their satin prom dresses with cheeky grins and silly poses. Chase had taken Holly to the senior dance wearing a pink tie that matched the color of her dress. He'd taken a lot of flak from the guys for it too. Paul Sebastian had been Abby's friendly escort. Though he'd been labeled by most of the students as nerdy, Abby had found him surprisingly quirky instead, enjoying his subtle sense of humor. Neither she nor Paul had been concerned with making a fashion statement. It had been nice just to have an official date.

She smiled at the memory despite the pain that pumped through her chest, threatening to implode that constantly beating organ with a simple gasp of breath. Holly had been her best friend, her confidant. A lone tear rolled down her cheek. "I miss her," she said.

"I know you do."

"I'm going to go see her this afternoon," Abby said with determination.

"Are you sure you're ready to do that?"

She looked her mother squarely in the eye and nodded. "It's long past time for me to face her."

"Do you want me to come with you?"

Abby shook her head. "No. You should go back to the hospital. I need to do this on my own."

Joyce Warren bit down on her lower lip but nodded her head. She met Abby's gaze with worry etched across her features. Abby prayed her mother would note the tension surrounding the subject and drop it. Thankfully, she did just that.

"I'll take my bags to my room when I get back," Abby said and turned toward the bright yellow kitchen. The time had come to deal with her past head on. She needed to do it now, before she lost her nerve.

⸺•《◉》•⸺

As Abby slid into the driver's seat of her red Acura, her lungs heaved with a heaviness she couldn't deflate. Why had she come back? What on earth had possessed her to believe she might be able to help? All she wanted to do was stomp down on the gas pedal and race out of town, leaving her painful memories deeply buried in the past. A past she could evade as long as she kept it at a distance. Avoidance had always seemed like a good strategy. Unfortunately, she'd never been very good at it. Besides, what she wanted to do and what she came here to do were two completely different things. She'd made promises, one to her mother and another to herself. This time she was determined to set things right before she left. The faster she succeeded, the faster she could leave. With a heavy, bone-weary breath, Abby shifted the car into reverse and backed out of the driveway.

The warm breeze blew through the limp strands of her dark hair, effectively drying the thin sheen of perspiration that had formed across the back of her neck. Abby drove east on Sycamore to First Street, turning right, she headed south. Ten blocks later, the tightly-knit population of houses began to scatter and melt away into vast acres of yellow-singed semi-harvested farmland. It was this rich, fertile land that solidly wrapped itself around the small community, leaving the town woven into a taut cocoon of unified civilization.

As far as places to grow up, Mills Pond had been a decent one. Abby's foundation had been shaped here. Her parents had bathed her in their love and instilled in her such genuine values as kindness, honesty and hard work. She had been an integral part of their family until that fateful day in early June, ten long years ago. It had been a regular day, one just like any other hot summer day in the Midwest. How had things gotten so out of control so quickly? One minute she was trying to calm Holly down by distracting her with the favored lyrics of a popular song by The Backstreet Boys and the next, they were standing on opposite sides of a line that neither one could cross.

Abby climbed a hill with the accelerator pressed to the floorboard. The road that would lead her toward Holly was fast approaching on the left. She slowed, made the turn and quickly heard the crunch of rock and grit beneath her tires as the asphalt gave way to gravel. She slowed the car to a crawl, following one curve and then another as she drove. It was a peaceful day; the sky was a deep azure, the green leaves in the massive old oak trees lining the roadway swayed silently from the breeze wafting across the flat Kansas plains. None of that helped to calm the wild staccato that was beating her heart to death. It had been so long. Why hadn't she come sooner? Would it have helped lessen some of the guilt, some of the grief she carried with her?

Abby parked the car in front of a small gardener's shed. Closing the door behind her, she tugged at the legs of her tan shorts and the back of her white T-shirt. Both were damp and sticking to her body. She brushed at a cluster of orange cat hairs that littered the hem of her shirt before noting the little building beside her. It looked sturdy enough to take on inclement weather. However, the gray paint covering the wooden siding was badly blistered and peeling. She stepped past it, beyond the overgrown blood red rose bushes and sturdy blocks of gray stone. Watching her footing on the uneven ground, she walked forward while the loud *thwack* of her flip-flops slapping the bottoms of her feet overpowered the sweet sounds of chirping birds nesting in the treetops high above.

Finally, she'd made it. Gingerly, she stepped toward the large beige marbled-stone marker in front of her. She swallowed hard as she read the inscription – *Holly Rebecca Miles, Beloved Daughter, Born April 14th, 1981 – Died June 2nd, 1999.* The tears Abby had held in for far too long sprang to her eyes like a leaky faucet, flooding her vision. Her heart broke into a thousand tiny pieces as she fell to her knees and wept.

Chapter Four

ABBY BREATHED IN a deep breath of air and was immediately assaulted by a string of memories from her youth—the scents of pine and varnish, the background sound of a saw in motion ripping a clean line through an unwieldy piece of plywood forcing a plume of fine sawdust powder to cling to everything around it. Her boots kicked through the evidence as she walked from the office to the front counter at Warren Lumber. She was happy to be here, away from the house. She'd barely escaped her mother's well-meaning update of her father's condition. She knew it was only a matter of time before he woke up, before she would be expected to make a bedside appearance. Waking in her childhood home, the regret she felt following her decade long defection had nearly smothered her. After her visit to Holly's gravesite yesterday, facing her father when she was far from prepared would push her over the edge of a cliff and into a dark abyss of emotion she wasn't sure she could manage.

She'd spent a restless night fighting off nightmares she'd thought were long ago forgotten, her subconscious rooting around for old footage of her prolonged friendship with Holly. The dreams had started with a beautiful rolling meadow on a bright summer day. Beneath a vast cloudless royal blue sky the two of them ran hand in hand, their peals of laughter dancing on the warm breeze shifting around them.

One of them brunette, the other blonde, running barefoot through the grass, their long curling strands of hair bouncing against their backs as they charged toward the thick sprawling patch of Black-Eyed Susan's. Before they could reach them, however, a thick swarm of angry bee's surrounded them, stinging their arms and legs as they fell to the ground covering their faces protectively with their hands. Abby had bolted upright in the dark swatting furiously at the imaginary swarm while a thick sheen of perspiration covered her entire body. It took everything she had to quiet the terror-filled screams loudly resounding in her ears. Even now, she nearly shuttered as she struggled with the images still lingering in her head.

"Hey Abby, it's great to see you."

Abby confirmed the tone of his voice matched the excited smile on his face. Charlie Newton had been the first person her parents had employed at Warren Lumber. She had only been five years old at the time and he had watched her grow up. He'd also been a witness to all those little temper tantrums she'd thrown when she'd wanted something and couldn't coerce her parents into granting her wish on moment's whim.

She gave him a huge smile and moved into position for the bear-hug she knew was coming. "Hi Charlie, it's good to see you," she said, barely able to get the words out before his strong arms depleted her current supply of oxygen.

He hadn't changed all that much over the years. He was nearly six-foot tall, lean and muscular, as fully noted by the solid grip of his embrace. He snickered at her muffled complaint as he bent backward, lifting her feet off the ground. There were still a few threads of brown peppering his thick gray hair. If memory served correctly, he'd had a few strands of gray lacing his dark mane and thick beard the last time she'd seen him. Now, his beard was closely cropped to his jaw and completely gray. His pale lavender eyes were dancing with mischief when he returned her feet to the floor.

"Welcome home."

Abby shook, trying to hide the smile threatening to overtake her features and failed miserably. "Thank you."

Charlie broke into a deep chuckle, obviously pleased with the result of his actions. "You always were easy to fluster. Guess you haven't grown out of that yet! It's a good thing to know."

"You behave yourself," Abby said, the warning in her voice not nearly ominous enough to deter him.

"Darlin," Charlie chuckled, his voice overt with a teasing edge, "you know better than to expect that from me!"

She smiled at him. What else could she do? She'd lost the battle before she'd known she was even part of it.

Looking downright delighted, he complained loudly. "Now look, you've made me forget what I came in here for."

"All right Charlie, quit your flirting. You've got work to do."

Abby recognized the voice of Donnie Burke, another long-time employee as he appeared at the end of aisle four, close to the front counter.

"Hi Donnie," Abby said, another smile crossing her flushed features as she took him in. Unlike Charlie's sturdy build, Donnie was large—all over. He had stock in both height and girth, along with a full head of jet-black hair that hung down partially covering his ears and nearly blinding him. It was obvious he needed a trim badly. He had dark cinnamon brown eyes—when you could see them—and a clean shaven face the color of salmon, though it tended to turn a darker shade of pink during happy hour.

"How ya doing, Squirt?"

Abby visibly cringed which brought another bout of laughter from both men. "Did you really have to remember that after all these years?"

Donnie masked his face with mock horror. "You mean to tell me that's not your name?"

Abby sputtered but found she was unable to form the words she wanted to use for her retort. This, of course, set off another round of rambunctious hoots, making Abby's face flame with embarrassment. The only thing that saved her from further humiliation was the intrusion of another body. A customer had entered the premises.

Turning her back on the ridiculous pair in front of her, Abby offered her attention to the newcomer. When her gaze met his, her heart nearly did a grueling catapult within her chest. Though aged from a youthful boy into a full grown man, his face was familiar at once. His amber eyes demanded her attention, making a more intimate critique of him impossible. She'd always felt inept and awkward around him, her current situation included. Without warning, her body exploded into an ice-cold sweat. As though sensing her trepidation, his lips formed into a relaxed smile, the left corner lifting slightly higher than the right.

As if to tamp down the invisible current seemingly overtaking the scant space between them, Donnie stepped forward and reached an arm toward the man, clasping his hand in a hearty shake. "Hey, Chad, how ya doin?"

Chad Austin stood only an arm-length away from her. He was a good three inches taller than Charlie, maybe more. His deep mahogany colored hair was neatly trimmed over his bronzed, sun-kissed face. His arms were darker yet, pleasantly revealed by the short sleeves of his pale blue T-shirt. They were muscular arms connected to a pair of large hands with long tapered fingers.

"I'm doing fine," Chad said. "How about yourself?"

Abby watched those very fingers disengage from the handshake.

Donnie looked in her direction and smiled before turning his attention back to Chad. "Doing great, thanks. But hey, since the boss is here," he nodded in her direction with a subtle jerk of his head, "Charlie and I had better get back to work."

Abby's face flushed an ever more damning pink. "I'm hardly the boss."

All three of the men broke into elated laughter before Charlie quickly followed Donnie toward the rear of the building, leaving Abby alone with Chad.

Once again, he extended the same relaxed smile on her as he had the moment before. For the second time in a matter of seconds, she felt a billion icy prickles break across her skin. No matter how cute or charming he was, he was the brother of her enemy. It couldn't get much worse than that.

"Hi, Abby," he said.

His voice was smooth as it flowed over her and she liked the way he said her name. She really needed to stop that line of thinking. A long time ago he'd been the focus of her admiration. Though she'd been smitten with him once, she would need to keep those feelings locked in the past as she was not about to let this go anywhere. Besides, she would be headed back to St. Louis soon so there was no cause to consider the reason he made her feel so rattled. She looked up into the soft golden brown of his eyes and fought off the desire to flinch, or melt, she wasn't sure which. "Hey, Chad."

He stared at her for a moment longer than necessary. "I was really sorry to hear about your dad."

She couldn't help feeling inept and awkward all over again. There was something about the way he looked at her that caught her off guard. She'd always thought it was because she was young and inexperienced. However, it was no longer the case. She was all grown up and he still had the same affect on her. Pulling her gaze away from his, she drew in a quick breath. "Thanks."

Still watching her, Chad laid the palm of his right hand on the gray laminate countertop and began tracing idle patterns with his index finger. "How long are you staying in town?"

Abby moved her gaze away from the easy movements of his

fingers to rest upon his features once again. "I suppose until my dad recovers enough for mom to come back to work."

"That's good."

"Why?"

He smiled. "It's always nice to see a friendly face around here. Especially one I haven't seen in a while."

"Right," she said.

"Have you had a chance to hook up with anyone from school yet?"

She shook her head. "No."

"Great! Let me take you out for a beer."

Abby knew her eyes flared wide as she acknowledged his offer. Could she have a beer with the enemy? No, Chase was the enemy, Chad was not. He hadn't even been around that horrible summer. Would it have made a difference if he had been? Would he have hated her too? "Thanks, but I don't think that's such a good idea."

He gave her a perplexed look. "Why not?"

"I don't think many people in town would approve."

His eyes flashed a deep liquid brown. "Abby Warren, why in the world would you say that?"

"I really don't have any friends left here."

He lifted his right hand from the countertop, bringing his fingers to rest beneath his chin. Looking down at the floor, he pondered her statement. After a brief pause he looked up at her again. "That's not true. You've got one standing right here."

"Chad, you really don't have any reason to be nice to me."

"I beg to differ," he said, an easy smile curving his lips while his arms crossed over the width of his chest. "I'd really like to buy you that beer for no other reason than to prove it to you."

"It's not necessary."

"Maybe not to you, but it is to me."

"Chad, for both of our sakes, please just leave it alone."

He smiled again. This was not the easy smile of a moment ago, but something of a more determined nature. "Not until you agree."

"I can't."

He took a step closer, invading her personal space. "Can't or won't?" he asked.

With a deep breath, Abby lifted her hand to her forehead and closed her eyes. She couldn't think with him standing so close. She could smell the fresh, earthy scent of him, a heady mix of cedar and sunshine. It was doing a good job of throwing her completely off-kilter.

His voice was velvet smooth when he spoke. "Which is it?"

She sighed heavily. "Both. Why does it matter?"

When she opened her eyes, he was viewing her with a keen, sharp gaze. "I thought we used to be friends."

She gave a quick, inward groan. All those years ago she'd wanted to be so much more. Why the attention now when she didn't want it? She couldn't afford to open herself up to anyone in Mills Pond. This town had crushed her without a backward glance and she wasn't willing to relive the experience all over again. "We were."

"So for old times sake," he said, flashing a smile that oozed with sex appeal. "What have you got to lose?"

She remembered the power of that particular smile and her beating heart pulsed faster within her chest. She was dumbfounded as to how he could still have such a major effect on her.

He dropped his arms and placed his hands on his hips, squarely meeting her gaze. Though no words were spoken, his intent came across loud and clear.

Abby's heart skipped a full beat, and then another. He was gorgeous and kind and she wanted to jump into her car with him and fly past the city limits, never looking back. She could imagine the heat pouring in through the windshield with a cooling breeze blowing through the open windows as they floored the accelerator and the scenery flew by. They could go anywhere, she didn't care. It didn't matter as long as Mills Pond was a distant speck in the rearview mirror.

"Just so you know, I'm going to stand here until you say yes."

Abby blinked, trying to dislodge the scene in her head as his words registered in her distracted brain. "Then you're going to have a long day ahead of you."

"It's one beer," he said, taking another step closer, maneuvering further into her personal space.

She felt the heat coming off him in waves. Her body froze to the spot where she stood facing him with uncertainty. "Why?" she whispered, barely breathing.

He looked her solidly in the eye. "I'd like to hear where life has taken you. Your parents told me that you're a professional artist. I saw some of your glass pieces at their house when I remodeled the kitchen and think they're absolutely beautiful."

Stunned that he knew such personal details about her life and that he had complimented her again after all these years on her current works of art, she wavered in her resolve. "You saw my work?"

"I always knew you were talented. You produced topnotch projects in school. It was a given that you'd be successful in whatever path you chose to pursue."

"Thanks," she said. She couldn't believe he remembered those stolen moments they'd shared together in the art room.

"So, how about that beer? I really am interested in learning more."

Abby swallowed the rock that had formed in her throat and nodded her head. "Okay."

He smiled at her again. "I'll pick you up at six?"

"I can just meet you there."

"Nonsense," he said, strolling away from her. "Here or your folks' house?"

Her voice stammered nervously as she gazed toward his retreating back. "How did you know I was staying with my folks?"

His soft chuckle reached her ears but he didn't turn around. "It's a small town."

Abby drew in a deep breath and shook her head. A major drawback to living in a small town was the fact that there was no privacy. Your business ultimately became everyone else's, whether intended or not. Regardless, letting him pick her up wasn't such a bad idea. At least she wouldn't be stuck waiting for him if she arrived before he did. The thought of sitting alone in that noisy, stuffy bar made her visibly cringe. Thank goodness he was focused on gathering supplies the next row over and didn't witness the motion. She wouldn't have wanted him to take her reaction the wrong way. "You can pick me up at my parents' house," she said, turning to face him.

He glanced up with that oh-so-charming grin plastered across his face. "Great," he said. "I'm looking forward to it."

She worked hard to swallow the lump that was suddenly blocking her airway. It had taken no effort at all on his part to sway her steadfast determination to refuse him. Had she completely lost her backbone? What in the world was wrong with her?

Chapter Five

DEADWOOD DICK'S BAR could definitely rival one of the popular bars in downtown St. Louis for happy hour. But then again, this was the only bar in Mills Pond. Abby supposed that was a big factor. She'd only been here a few times in her younger years with her parents. Usually on a Friday night when her mother hadn't wanted to cook and her father needed to blow off some steam by knocking back a few cold ones.

She tried to ignore the curious stares when she walked through the door, Chad following closely behind. He pointed to the last available table, a high-top nestled between two dart machines and the first of three pool tables, all of which were in use. Classic Bad Company blared from a huge jukebox in the corner to her right. It was darker inside the building than she'd expected with the abundance of wood paneling and lack of windows. The florescent lighting flickering annoyingly overhead didn't help matters either.

"What would you like?" Chad asked, bending down so the warmth of his breath brushed her ear when he spoke.

"Whatever you're having is fine."

When he nodded his head in response, she moved away from him toward the open table feeling several sets of eyes upon her as she walked. *Ah, the defector returns to face another round of ridicule.* She could already hear the gossip spreading beyond the four walls of the bar. By tomorrow morning, everyone in town would know that she was back.

Sliding onto a stool near the wall, she took a deep breath and tried her best to soothe her jumbled nerves. Glancing up, she saw Chad standing in front of a bar that took up the entire east wall of the building. She could see his reflection in the long line of mirrors behind it. He smiled and then laughed as he exchanged words with someone she didn't recognize occupying the stool next to him. Also reflected in the mirrors was a mammoth mess of brightly lit and blinking beer signs. If you stared long enough, the strobe of wildly flickering colors could make you nauseous. An assortment of glasses and mugs hung from wooden inserts built into the ceiling. Just below the mirrors sat bottle after bottle of booze. All you had to do was name your poison.

From where she sat, the music sounding from the jukebox was muffled by the noise from the crowd. People were everywhere, standing two-deep at the bar, crammed around the varied collection of tables, and casually gathered about the brightly lit pool tables. She met the gaze of one such patron as she scanned the scene before her. With a bottle of Miller in one hand, a pool stick in the other, he smiled at her. Obviously he had yet to hear the scandalous chitchat now freely spreading throughout the premises.

"Hope Bud Light's all right?" Chad asked, handing her a cold brown bottle.

She nodded, pulling her gaze away from the pool table and looking up into his handsome face. "Yes, it's fine, thanks."

He smiled and settled onto the stool directly across from her. "So, is it as bad as you thought?"

She smiled back. "Worse."

He put his hand over his heart. "Ouch."

"Sorry," she said. "I guess it's not that much different than the bars in St. Louis."

"Do you like living there?" he asked.

"It's okay. I have a loft downtown. Well, at least for the time being."

"What does that mean?"

"They've acquired new building management and raised the rent to something I can't afford. I have a month to find something else."

"So you're moving?"

"That's the plan though I'm having trouble finding something suitable within my budget. I need the open space a loft offers to accommodate my art studio. A regular apartment just doesn't work. Trust me, I've tried."

"Maybe that's a sign," he said.

"For what?"

"That it's time to move somewhere else?"

Abby hadn't considered that option. She'd moved to St. Louis following college and had been there for the past six years. She had a couple of close female friends, but really didn't date much. People found her work, or at least her work schedule, intimidating. She was artistic, not eccentric. It meant that she wasn't stuck with an eight-to-five work week. In fact, she was free to work all hours of the day or night. Whenever an idea struck, her passion flared, forcing her into a creative zone. When she hit that intensity level, everything else ceased to matter. Her attention became fully imprisoned and she was driven to complete the piece no matter how long it took. She couldn't recall how many dates she'd stood up, however unintentional, causing any attempt at romance to fizzle before ever having had a chance to begin. She shrugged her shoulders noncommittally. "Maybe."

"Hey, Chad, who've you got here?" A tall, dark-headed man said, stepping up to the table.

"Hey, Darren!" Chad greeted cheerfully. "Do you remember Abby Warren?"

A set of dark eyes met her gaze. Under the dim lighting, she couldn't tell what color they were. He smiled at her. "You were a year behind us, right?"

Abby smiled carefully, nodding her head.

"Your parents own the lumberyard?" he said, but it came out as more of a confirmation than a question.

"Yes," she said.

"I was sorry to hear about your dad's accident."

"Thanks," she replied as she met Chad's gaze across the table.

"Abby, this is Darren Rustin. We played football together in high school. He's the manager at Montgomery's Hardware," he said.

Darren held out his hand and she slid her palm against his in natural greeting. "Nice to see you again," he said.

Abby remembered him briefly. They hadn't had anything in common but she knew for certain that he hadn't been part of Chase Austin's group.

"Well I'm headed over to hustle a little pool," Darren announced. "You wanna play?"

Chad met Abby's gaze before looking up at Darren. "Maybe later," he said.

"Yeah, right." Darren chuckled. "Abby, you're welcome to play too."

"Thanks." She laughed lightly and flashed her eyes in Chad's direction. She'd never played pool in her life and with this crowd, she wasn't about to start.

"All right then, catch ya later," Darren said, and with another light chuckle, turned his back to them and walked toward the crowd gathered around the pool tables.

"Sorry about that," Chad said when he was out of range to overhear.

Abby tipped her beer up for the last taste of bitter liquid. She looked at the empty bottle as though the brown glass had cracked and her drink had leaked out all over the table. There was no way that she'd already downed the entire beer. "No problem."

"How about another?" he asked, pointing toward her empty bottle.

She was here, she might as well stay. Besides, she was enjoying Chad's company a little more than she thought she ought to. She nodded her head, but vowed to slow her alcohol intake. The last thing she wanted to do was to make more of a fool out of herself than she already was.

When he left the table, she felt her false sense of security deflate. It was as if his physical presence offered some invisible barrier of protection between her and everyone else. She glanced around the room. The curious stares had dwindled. She fixed her gaze on Darren who was standing at the far pool table talking to someone with a familiar face. Searching her memory, she realized it was Karl Dunkin. He was still a big hulk of a guy with a kind face and pale green eyes. When Darren smiled and waved at her, she flushed with embarrassment but gave a quick flip of her hand before quickly diverting her gaze.

Sweeping her eyes away from the pool crowd, Abby located Chad at the bar locked in tense conversation with another male. His stance was stiff, shoulders drawn back, jaw taut. Whomever he was talking to was aggressively mouthing words she couldn't interpret from this distance. Chad turned his back to her in order to grab two full bottles of beer from the bartender. Turning to face the other man once again, he waved one of the bottles in a dismissive fashion and with long, quick strides, strode back toward their table.

As the man turned his head to watch Chad's retreat, his gaze locked with hers which caused her stomach to lurch painfully. Chad had been arguing with his brother. An older, more mature version of the boy she'd known glared daggers at her from across the room. She was certain he would like nothing better than to pierce her heart with multiple blades of steel many times over.

"Sorry about that," Chad said when he reached the table. "Chase is being a pain in the-you-know-what."

"Chase." She all but squeaked.

He handed her one of the cold beers. "Yeah. But don't worry about him."

"He doesn't like me much."

"Why?" he asked, clearly puzzled. "You were such good friends in high school."

"Oh, come on," she said, her tone skeptic.

"What are you talking about?"

Abby stared at Chad in bewilderment. Was he truly oblivious to the circumstances behind her abrupt departure from Mills Pond? Did he not know how cruel Chase and his cronies had been to her all those years ago?

"Abby?"

She rapidly blinked her eyes in order to clear her thoughts, to reconnect to the situation at hand. "It doesn't matter."

His body snapped forward and he reached his palm across the tabletop, gently placing it over the top of her hand. "Yes it does."

She felt the warmth of his touch, the tenderness of the action, and tears began to well in her eyes.

"Abby, talk to me. Please?"

She shook her head. Glancing around the room like a frightened doe, she located Chase once again. He was standing with his back toward them, a glass of dark amber liquid in his hand as he talked with Karl and Darren. The only indication of his anger could be noted in his agitated stance. The group around him seemed unaware of the tense exchange that had occurred between the brothers. Instead, they were teasing a tiny long-haired blonde at the pool table. With a pool stick in one hand, she waved a green bill in the air with the other.

Abby felt like an intruder watching them. Her life was so far removed from this place and the last thing she wanted was to cause problems for Chad. Lifting the bottle to her lips, she chugged down half the beer. When her hand began to tremble, she sat it back on the table. "I need to go," she said.

Chad looked over his shoulder. Abby was certain he followed the line of her gaze, honing in on Chase's form like he had a huge target on his back. When he turned his attention toward her once again, he shook his head. "Sure," he said, setting his empty beer bottle on the table and standing up. "Let's get out of here."

As she slid off her stool he stepped up beside her and wrapped an arm around her shoulders. Her pounding heart jumped for joy, overshadowing her dread for a quick moment before he led her out of the crowded bar and into the stifling heat of the early evening.

He'd watched Abby Warren walk through the door with Chad following directly behind her. That was a sick twist of events. Chad had pointed out an empty table along the back wall and they'd parted ways. While Chad ordered drinks, his attention bounced back and forth between the two. Chad was all smiles and chatter while Abby sat alone appearing extremely uneasy. But then again, why wouldn't she? Mills Pond was no longer her home. When Chad arrived at the table, he observed their casual banter and the deep seething anger began to build, slowly setting his chest on fire.

It was obvious that Chad was captivated by Abby. You only had to watch their exchange to see the way he smiled at her, the way she held his attention. This could not be happening. She would not be allowed to attach herself to this town again or anyone in it. He would stop her. He slammed his Jack and Coke down and held up the empty glass for the bartender to see. The color red began to creep into his peripheral vision, hazy, yet growing bolder as it continued to taint his view. He had to find a way to push her away from his family and friends. He had to shield them as he protected himself. He would not give her an opportunity to unearth his past; a past he'd managed to bury a long time ago. He vowed that one way or another, she would leave Mills Pond permanently.

Chapter Six

CHAD BREATHED IN a deep breath as the bar door slammed shut behind him, pushing the stale, smoky air out of his lungs and replacing it with a fresh round. His arm was solidly draped around Abby's shoulders, pulling her smaller frame against his larger one. He was afraid she was going to bolt before he had the ability to dissect the situation. They walked to his truck in silence as he carefully deciphered the best course of action. Opening the passenger door, he helped her climb in.

With keys in hand, he walked around the rear of the truck and cautiously slid into the driver's seat. Glancing over at her, his brow creased with worry. She stiffened and quickly turned her head to view the packed parking lot through the windshield. The tension bouncing between them was so thick he could cut it with a knife. "Will you tell me what's going on?" he asked, trying his best to keep the exasperation he felt from betraying him.

He watched as she pursed her lips but stayed silent. Her hands were clasped so tightly together on her lap that her knuckles were white; she was cutting off her circulation. Her shoulders began to tremble slightly and she closed her eyes. He could hear the abnormal rhythm of her breathing. It was as though her false bravado was about to crumble. He felt helpless and frustrated because he had no idea what was going on. He had no clue how to help her. Drawing in a ragged breath, he squeezed his fist around the set of metal in his hand, feeling the rough grooves of the keys biting into his palm. With as gentle a voice as he could muster, he spoke. "Abby, look at me."

When she did as he asked, he noted her clenched jaw. Her chin quivered as she blinked back unshed tears. Though he couldn't distinguish the color of her eyes in the darkened cab, he knew from experience the fiery aqua heat that was now burrowing into his own liquid amber stare. She closed her eyes again and drew in an agitated breath. He watched with fascination as she swallowed, breathed, and swallowed a second time. Finally, she spoke. "Would you please just take me home?"

A piercing pain slammed into his gut. "No." He uttered as he drew in a harsh breath of air.

She sighed and looked down at her lap. "It's better this way."

"I'm not taking you home until you level with me. This involves my brother and I think I have the right to know what's going on."

Her head snapped up and she fastened her intense gaze on him from across the cab. "You should probably ask him."

Chad drew in another deep breath and held it for a long moment before releasing. "I love my brother," he said, turning his head toward her so that he could gage how his words were received. "But honestly, I don't always trust his judgment. Something is vitally wrong here. I feel like you've been hurt and I need to know why."

"It was a long time ago."

"Maybe so, but the fallout isn't over. I feel like something blatant and ugly is going on right under my nose."

"You really don't know," she said as her facial features settled into a look of pure surprise.

"No." He groaned out loud. "I have no idea what just happened in there."

She met his flustered gaze again and sighed. "All right."

"You'll tell me?"

She nodded her head. "Yes, but I need a drink first." Then she pointed her index finger at the bar. "And I'm not going back in there."

"Okay," he said as a hesitant smile pulled at the corners of his mouth. "I know just the place."

Chad turned the key in the ignition and the truck rumbled to life. She glanced out the window as he shifted gears and maneuvered out of the parking lot. A heavy angst hung in the air while they drove down the highway in silence. He had a feeling they were about to dive into a conversation he wasn't sure he wanted to have. Not for his sake as he really wanted to know what was going on, but he wasn't sure Abby was ready to share anything with him. Intuition told him she'd been hurt badly. Her body language confirmed it. She sat quietly staring out the windshield with her arms folded tightly over her chest. He suddenly remembered how reserved she'd been in her youth. He was going to have to convince her that he wasn't the enemy. However, from the look of things, that might be easier said than done.

He drove through town and headed in a southwest direction toward Mills Pond. Actually it was more of a lake than the pond it started out to be when the town was founded. It had been dug out and expanded in the late 1940's, including the addition of a half-mile long dam. The south corner of the dam was a perfect fishing spot. A few hundred yards beyond that, the rocky beach twisted back and snaked east, creating a nice, semi-private swimming hole. He was familiar with both and had to fight to keep the smile off his face when he thought about taking Abby there.

The truck bounced lightly when the paved road turned into gravel. Within a few hundred feet it curved north, away from the lake. He felt Abby's gaze on him but stared straight ahead, trying his best to keep his attention on the dusty terrain in front of them. Attention avoidance was more for her benefit than his, but he failed miserably. Wanting to make sense of the ample range of emotion playing across her features, he turned his head for a quick appraisal before shifting his concentration back toward the rocky road in front of them. "I'm taking you to my house," he said. "It's out of the way and quiet. No one will bother us there."

"Oh, okay," she whispered quietly.

Finally, he began to slow. There was a gravel driveway ahead of them on the right. He turned the truck onto the drive and plowed straight ahead. After a couple hundred feet of choppy field and crunching rock, a clearing opened before them and a nice sized rustic two-story log cabin came into view, complete with a wide front porch. Huge, majestic oak trees dotted the green manicured lawn giving off plenty of shade. Turtle creek snaked behind them, curving ever so slightly around the house toward the north. Chad pulled onto the cement slab in front of the side garage and stopped.

"This is yours?" Abby asked, amazement reflecting in her gaze.

Chad nodded and turned his head to grace her with an ardent smile. "I built it myself."

Despite the current situation, she grinned. "Impressive."

He chuckled at her honest candor. "Why, thank you. You're not the only one with artistic talents."

————)•(()•(————

Abby laughed lightly and opened the truck door. Jumping to the ground she nearly toppled over as the hem of her blue jeans caught between her heel and the top of her sandal. She yanked it free before walking into the oversized garage Chad had opened by remote entry.

He strolled up beside her, briefly brushing her hand in passing. "Come on," he said with a bob of his head, "I'll show you around."

As her hand tingled from his touch, she nodded and followed him inside. The house smelled of cedar. An element she loved immediately and it brought a smile to her lips. She now knew why the scent gently clung to him. Walking through the large laundry room, they stepped into a huge kitchen. Unlike the blinding yellow of her mother's kitchen, his was pale cream in color. The cabinetry was cedar and absolutely beautiful. Moving her gaze, she noted the entire back wall of the house hosted floor to ceiling windows with a perfect view of the creek and woods beyond. The fusing kaleidoscope of pink, orange and yellow from the setting sun was a spectacular view to behold. A huge sliding glass door folded back into the wall and opened into a fully furnished screened-in porch that led to a sprawling deck. It was breathtaking; she'd never seen anything like it.

The dining area, complete with a dark pine table and oversized chairs extended off the kitchen and shared the dramatic window view. Both rooms swept into a huge space complete with vaulted ceilings and an open sitting-room on the second level that overlooked the living room in front of her. It also exhibited the biggest stone fireplace she'd ever seen. There was the perfect mix of stones that were different shapes, sizes, and colors with a thick cedar mantle that ran across the entire expanse, directly at eye level. There was a room to her left just before the base of the downward staircase that looked as though he used it for office space. The upward staircase was wide and had a solid, yet intricate cedar railing that led to the rooms above. He'd combined different tones of blues and greens with a few reds and yellows into the space, giving it a definite masculine feel.

"Bedrooms upstairs?" she asked.

He nodded his head in confirmation. "There are four bedrooms and three bathrooms. The master has a sitting area with a fireplace, an enormous walk-in closet, and a large master bath with a jetted tub. It also has its own balcony just above the back windows. There's a game room downstairs with a large screen television and seating area, a pool table, and a built-in bar."

She took another long look around before swinging her body back to face his. Putting her hands on her hips, she smiled. "Chad, it's absolutely gorgeous."

He was standing near the bar which separated the kitchen from the living room. "Thanks. Now, how about that drink?"

She nodded her head and walked toward him. Pulling out a heavy wooden stool, she climbed up and sat down on the large leather padded seat. He grabbed a couple of bottles of Bud Light from the refrigerator, along with a bottle of Crown Royal and a couple of shot glasses from a nearby cabinet. Her eyebrows wrenched upward as he set them in front of her. "Shots?" she asked.

He shrugged his shoulders as he left the kitchen and walked around the bar, sliding onto the stool beside hers. "I wasn't sure what you meant by *drink*," he said in his defense.

"Oh." She mouthed more than said aloud.

She met his gaze, certain her nervousness showed across her features. He turned his face away, opened the bottle of Crown Royal and filled the shot glasses. "Here," he said, sliding one in front of her.

Gazing down at his offering, she was certain she was going to need something to get through this. She just wasn't convinced that the choice of hard liquor was a sane decision. When he lifted his glass in a toast, she did the same, tapping her glass against his.

"Cheers," he said with a smile and tossed the drink back as if it was water. She looked from his face to her glass and back to his face before lifting the drink to her lips to take a sip. A thimble full of dark amber liquid burned as it slid down her throat. Her eyes began to water and she noted her glass was still nearly filled.

"It's easier if you drink it fast."

Without thinking about it, she swallowed the rest in one big gulp, the heat from it trailing down her body like a burning ember fully ignited.

He twisted the cap off one of the beer bottles and handed it to her. She grabbed it quickly and tipped it back hoping the cold liquid would help soothe the burning sensation the Crown Royal had left behind.

His face distorted awkwardly as he tried to hold back a smile that threatened to break free. "Better?" he asked.

Her throat to her stomach still burned but she nodded her head.

He twisted off the cap of the second bottle and leaned against the back of his stool taking a long, slow pull from the beer. "Okay, talk to me," he said.

Abby took a deep breath to settle her nerves. The stool pivoted and she turned so that she was facing him. His facial features were drawn tight as he gave her his full attention. She tried to focus on his face instead of the thick column of his neck, the width of his shoulders, or the way his immaculate white T-shirt hugged his body. His long, jean covered legs were spread apart, allowing her smaller, shorter ones in between. While the heels of his boots hooked over the wooden rungs of his stool, hers hung loosely between them. Gazing into his light brown eyes, she began to tell her story. "I'm sure you know what happened the summer Chase and I graduated?"

He nodded soberly. "Your friend Holly Miles was killed in a car accident."

Tears sprung to her eyes and she nodded her head. "Did you know that I was driving?"

"Yes. But it was an accident, right?"

Abby pursed her lips and shook her head sadly.

Angling his upper body toward her, he moved his hand to lightly caress her knee in quiet support. "Abby, tell me what happened."

"A week after graduation, Holly and Chase had a huge fight. They'd talked about going to the University of Oklahoma together but Holly had decided that after two years of dating exclusively, she needed some space. She wanted to go to nursing school at Rockhurst University in Kansas City. Chase was furious when she told him and he blamed me because I'd planned to attend the Kansas City Art Institute. After an explosive argument she showed up at my house in tears. To calm her down, we drove around for a while in her car and ended up at a party out at Mills Pond. She had a bottle of Bacardi stuffed under the car seat that she'd smuggled out of her parents' liquor cabinet. It was the hard stuff too."

With his eyes never leaving hers, he nodded his head and gently squeezed his fingers over her kneecap, urging her to continue.

"Holly proceeded to get wasted. I knew she was upset, especially after her Chase-bashing got bad. Guilt set in then and she cried hysterically for being mean. There is nothing worse than an emotional drunk girl."

Chad chuckled lightly but declined to comment further.

"As soon as Chase showed up, Holly took off into the woods to relieve her bladder."

Chad smiled at her choice of wording.

She smiled back. "I'm trying to be considerate as I recount the situation. Anyway," she said, waving her hand in the air, "she was gone a long time. Chase tried to quiz me about Holly's decision but I refused to talk to him. It wasn't my business and I'd promised myself that I'd stay out of it. He finally got bored and took off. When Holly didn't come back, several of us split up to search for her."

"What happened?" Chad prodded.

"I found her curled up and half concealed by a couple of large bushes not far from where the car was parked. At first I thought she'd gotten disoriented or lost but when she sat up, I saw the dark red welt underneath the dirt on her tear-streaked face and her torn clothing." Abby gasped a quick breath as she pictured the scene in her head. "It wasn't nature that attacked her."

"Was Holly hurt?" Chad asked in a soft, respectful tone.

Abby met his gaze squarely and fought back tears. Slowly, she nodded her head. "Someone at that party, someone from Mills Pond, took advantage of my best friend." For some reason, she couldn't say the word *rape* out loud. It was stuck in her throat, even after all these years.

"Did she tell you who was responsible?"

Abby shook her head. "Holly was in shock and never said a word to anyone. We'll never know the truth. I'm not sure how it happened but the DNA evidence was deemed contaminated so whoever attacked her got away with it."

Chad closed his eyes briefly. When their gazes met again he nodded his head. "What happened after you found her?"

"A couple of girls helped me get her into the car. She was shivering so I rolled up the windows and turned on the heat even though it was warm outside. While I was driving, a song we liked came on the radio so I turned it up and started singing the lyrics, hoping it would distract her. Out of nowhere, someone's high beams flashed in the rearview mirror and a vehicle swerved all over the road behind us. They were driving too fast and appeared to be out of control as they quickly caught up." Her breath became wedged in her chest as the terror she'd survived over a decade ago seeped into her bones all over again. She had to fight to breathe.

The horror of the memory must have been etched across her face because Chad jerked his hand from her knee to caress her cheek, his fingers lightly grazing her skin. "Abby, it's okay," he said, clenching his jaw. She could read within his features, the fear of where her story was headed.

She shook her head, tears spilling down her face. "No, it isn't. I slowed down thinking it was Chase following us back into town but whoever it was kept moving closer, almost bumping the car. I tried to get out of the way but there was nowhere to go. The tires hugged the edge of the road on the passenger side for a few seconds and I thought I might be able to maintain control. Before I knew it, the car jerked sharply toward the ditch and we were flying into the foliage headed nose-first down a steep embankment, hitting everything in our path along the way. The car ended up on its right side, partially wrapped around a tree. I had my seatbelt on but still managed to hit my head on the steering wheel. Everything went black. When I woke, the seatbelt was still fastened and holding me in place. I looked toward Holly and confirmed she was buckled in but she was frighteningly still. I thought she'd blacked out as well until I saw the broken branch that had smashed through window. The ragged end had struck her in the head. I tried to talk to her to get her to respond but she wouldn't answer so I reached over to tap her on the shoulder. Her head rolled to the side then, eyes wide open, and I knew something was horribly wrong. I don't remember screaming but I must have because my throat was raw for days afterward. I guess it could have been from the various interrogations I encountered as well. They made me repeat the grueling ordeal over and over again.

"I realized years later that they'd been looking for inconsistencies in my story. Grasping that insight didn't change anything though. Holly was still gone." She gulped a huge breath of air trying to curtail the excess emotion churning in her chest. "To this day, I still feel guilty."

He tenderly lifted her chin with his fingers. "It's not your fault," he said, a fierce intensity burning in his gaze.

She shook her head. "I miss Holly, Chad. After all these years, my heart still aches for her loss."

"How could it not?"

She met his gaze squarely, ready to share the burden of her grief in its deepest, darkest form. "The guilt I carry with me comes from a position of utter selfishness," she said. "I'm ashamed to admit I felt relieved that I was the one driving. If Holly had been behind the wheel that night, my parents would have had to bury me. I feel terrible that she died and that her family eventually moved away from Mills Pond, but also thankful that I don't have to face them." Her body began to tremble uncontrollably with the admission of the innate shame she'd held fast to all those years and her tears fell even harder.

Chad's boots hit the solid wood flooring with a loud thud as he stood. Reaching for her, his arms wrapped snuggly around her while he pulled her against him. His fingers tangled within the long strands of her hair as he spoke. "Sweetheart, it's okay. Those are human emotions, the same anyone would feel in such a circumstance," he murmured as she buried her face in his immaculate white shirt. While she felt those horrible memories from her past wash over her, he stroked her back with one hand while he held her head firmly against his chest with the other. He continued to embrace her, to soothe her with words of comfort and support until the shudders finally subsided and she could breathe again without her chest heaving.

Once he let her go, he poured two more shots of Crown Royal, handing one to her. She belted hers down as soon as she had it in her hand.

"Whoa, girl," he said, a tight smile crossing his lips.

Stifling a hiccup, she looked at him with huge eyes and tear-rimmed lashes. "Sorry."

"No apologies necessary."

"Thank you."

He nodded his head as he chugged his own drink down. Setting his glass on the counter, he slid his body onto the bar stool opposite her once again and met her gaze. "Abby," he said, stroking his thumb along the line of her jaw. "How does Chase fit into all of this? His reaction toward you at the bar tonight still doesn't make sense."

Abby drew in a deep breath, her body quaking anew as angst washed through her. "The police couldn't prove the existence of the other vehicle. There were no decipherable tracks on the road, no witnesses, and no one ever came forward. Chase called me a liar, among other things, and blamed me for Holly's death."

Chad swore aloud, the words quiet, yet subtle.

"Holly's toxin-screen indicated her blood alcohol level was well over the legal limit but mine proved that I was stone-cold sober. Because of that, they ruled it an accident. My innocence didn't matter to Chase though. I think he needed someone to hold responsible and I was the easiest target."

"Abby, I'm so sorry."

She lifted her gaze to his and held it. "Do you remember the saying, *sticks and stones may break my bones but words will never hurt me?*"

He nodded his head. "Yes."

"It's wrong. You can heal from broken bones. Words, however, can be so much worse because the mental abuse inflicted can long outlast physical trauma, especially when it comes from people you thought you could trust. Chase turned the people I thought were my friends against me. Their harsh words and dismissive attitude were more than I could stand. In a very short period of time, they stole my sense of worth and proceeded to tear a hole through my family's foundation. I left town vowing never to come back."

"Until now," he said. His voice was soft and empathic.

Looking down at her lap, she nodded sadly. "I had to. My parents needed me."

Again, Chad placed his fingers beneath her chin and lifted her face so that she would look at him. His rich amber gaze bored into hers. "Abby, I am so sorry for everything you've been through. Chase was wrong then and he's wrong now."

"Whether he was wrong or not doesn't change anything."

"Maybe not the past, but the future can change." The warm pad of his thumb gently traced the delicate curve of her chin. "I'm going to make you a promise."

"What kind of promise can you make when this has nothing to do with you?" she asked skeptically.

"I'll do whatever I can to help you sort this out. Abby, you won't have to go through this on your own."

"Why would you do that?"

He smiled. Bending forward, he gently brushed his lips across her forehead. They were soft, the rush of his accompanying breath warm. "Because I was stupid enough to let you go once," he said, cupping her face between his palms. When her eyes met his, she could see the steely determination set in the crease of his brow. "I won't to do it again."

His words surprised her. "What are you talking about?"

He chuckled lightly as he dropped his hands. "Abby, I was crazy about you in high school. I loved the fact that you were dedicated to your passion. You were so driven to improving your talent, so focused on becoming the person you were meant to be rather than fighting for a place within the highly flawed social pecking order of our little podunk high school. You continually amazed me and I was drawn to the art room day after day just to be near you. I knew with your incredible gifts, you'd be successful. And I was right. I just wish I'd had the nerve then to tell you how I felt. Especially after learning everything you've gone through. I could have been there when you needed me the most."

His words slowly sunk in. There had been something between them all those years ago and neither had had the courage to speak up. High school kids could be so fickle, so cruel when they weren't able to get what they wanted. She'd seen more than one tortured soul in those days, herself included. But she should have known that Chad Austin would be different. She did know. She just hadn't trusted her own instincts.

Gazing into his handsome face, his dark hair grew hazy and she had to blink back the river of tears that threatened to spill. However this time, hope and joy fused with the pain of her past. With his support, could things really change? Was it possible? Could she truly find a reason to once again call Mills Pond home?

Chapter Seven

A THICK, WARM breeze blew through the open window as Chad drove his pickup down the blacktop road toward home. The inky blackness of the early morning hour seeped in around him more than usual. The bright golden twinkle of stars spread across his windshield had lost their normal appeal. His mind was absorbed in the tragic story Abby Warren had shared with him. Although he'd dropped her off at her parent's house only a few short moments ago, he could still feel her presence in the cab. If he tried hard enough, he was sure he would catch the faint scent of her honeysuckle shampoo. He groaned. The last thing he'd wanted to do was to let her out of his sight.

He gripped the steering wheel as her words played over and over in his mind. Whoever had forced her off the road had also attacked Holly Miles. He was sure of it. As a result, Abby's best friend had been killed and his own brother had viciously harassed her until she'd been compelled to flee. Chad had been enrolled at Oklahoma State University at the time. Though it was summer, he'd decided to take a couple of additional classes. Well, at least that's what he'd told his parents. He did take the classes but the real reason he'd stayed was his interest in a certain female student. Leigh Stratton had been a year older than he with a penchant for intellect and a passion for nude models. It wasn't necessarily her artistic interpretation associated with her models that made her wildly popular, but what she rewarded them with. While he'd spent the summer engaging in extra-curricular activities—which ended well before the fall semester began—Abby's world had fallen apart.

If he hadn't let his libido get the best of him and come home that summer, would it have made a difference? He'd like to think so. He could have defended her at the very least. He knew there was truth in her words, he'd felt them in his bones. He'd also seen the anger and blame Chase held fast to. Back then, would he have been able to defy his brother to protect an innocent girl—a girl he was crazy about? In reality, it no longer mattered how things may have played out. A decade of broken dreams and grief had festered. He'd felt her pain and frustration cut through him. Her sobbing body wrapped in his arms had nearly been more than he could stand. What she'd gone through made his heart ache, propelling him past his fear of rejection. Instead, he was determined to make up for lost time and set things straight. She needed him now more than ever before.

———— ⫸《◉》⫷ ————

Abby lay in the middle of her bed staring unblinkingly up at the ceiling. The sun was beginning to rise but she wanted nothing to do with it. She was still in awe that she had spilled her dark secrets to Chad Austin the night before. All she'd done was open her mouth and everything she'd held back for so long tumbled right into his lap. No easing into it for her. She groaned out loud, wondering if the morning light would bring a change of heart. Last night he'd viewed her as a wounded girl in need of defending. Would daylight bring clarity and distort that point of view? Instead of a broken soul, would he perceive her as a crackpot unworthy of saving? She knew it would be wise to keep her distance but his admission had caught her off-guard. Could there still be something between them after all these years?

Her body tingled as she remembered the steel-band of his arm around her shoulders, the firm grip of his hand on her knee, and his lips, warm and full, brushing across her forehead. His amber eyes had burned into hers like molten lava, shimmering embers of collected heat, both pained and feral. He had witnessed her grief first-hand and tendered absolution. Refusing to let her carry the heavy burden of those past offenses singlehandedly, he'd gathered her into his arms and offered comfort. He had wanted to be her champion. At least he had wanted to last night.

Abby couldn't believe that he'd been attracted to her all those years ago. Though she'd been extremely shy and awkward, she had longed for him in the worst way. Never considering there could be a real spark between them she'd kept her crush a secret. She never even confided in Holly. All those afternoons he'd sat with her in the art room absorbed in one project or another had only been a ploy to be near her. Chad Austin football star, Chad Austin homecoming king, Chad Austin reserved artist had been hiding a little secret of his own. The tingle turned into a full-body tremble. She felt faint, yet exuberant. Hope swelled within her chest. She could never have imagined this sudden turn of events and fervently hoped the light of day only intensified his yearning, especially after he'd asked to see her again.

Looking around the room, she felt a twinge of déjà vu. Her bedroom had been left the same as the day she'd abandoned it. The comforter on her bed was still the girly pink and purple flowery mess that matched the curtains hanging over twin windows. Well, except for the blob of heaping orange fur parked at the end of her mattress. The headboard, dresser, and desk had been painted white with a stenciled pattern of purple flowers painted on their tops. Her youthful paintings and drawings, now slightly faded, hung on one wall solidly affixed to the corkboard behind it. A vinyl purple bean-bag chair sat on the floor in the corner next to the stereo stand. She'd spent hours sitting there listening to her favorite albums and cassettes with sketchpad in hand. An eclectic collection of paperback books sat neatly on the shelf above the desk amid an array of memento's from her childhood. She couldn't believe her parents hadn't converted the room into storage, workout space, or anything that would be a less painful reminder of her absence.

The orange princess phone tucked into a shelf on her headboard rang, forcing her to jump at the intrusion. It had affected not only her but Brewtus as well. He gave a half-clipped squall, met her gaze with a perturbed look and jumped from the bed. He was sitting on the floor staring at the closed door with his back to her when the phone rang a second time. It was early; the sun was barely up. Who on earth would call at this hour? She hurried to grab it before it woke her mother. With a voice gruff from nonuse, she answered. "Hello?"

There was no response from the other end, just as there was no dial tone to indicate the caller had disconnected.

"Hello?" She repeated.

Still, there was no reply to her address, only the empty silence of dead air connecting her to the caller on the opposite end of the line.

Growing slightly frustrated, she sat up. "Is anyone there?" she asked.

The sound that greeted her was a loud, solid click made from the now severed connection.

Hanging up the receiver, she grumbled as she crawled out of bed, nearly stumbling over the pile of discarded toy animals she'd tossed off the mattress the night before. Breaking her leg would certainly not work out well in her favor. And though she wasn't a superstitious person, she hoped this was not an omen as to how the rest of her day was going to pan out.

"Come on Brewtus," she said as she tugged on a pair of polka dot lounging pants to accompany the wrinkled pink T-shirt she'd slept in. "Let's go fix some coffee and open a can of Fancy Feast. It looks like today may be a long one."

———— ◦《◉》◦ ————

Hanging up the receiver, he felt a rush of adrenaline and smiled. The call had woken her up. Good. Her voice had been low and sultry in his ear. The type of voice he could imagine on the opposite end of a service call—a sex service call. He numbered a sheet of paper from one to ten and started jotting down ideas that came to mind, things that he could do to assure she wouldn't stay in Mills Pond long. He certainly didn't like the company she was keeping and planned to put a stop to it as quickly as possible. With some precise premeditated pressure, he was sure it wouldn't take long to sway Chad's interest away from Abby Warren.

Besides, what did Abby truly have to offer? She was a looker, he'd give her that. She always had been. The darkness of his past began seeping back into his head and he quickly wondered what it would have been like to have cornered Abby in those woods instead of Holly Miles. Holly had been outgoing and sweet. Blonde hair and blue eyes aside, she'd had a cute, petite body that had captured a lot of attention. Abby on the other hand was taller and much curvier. In the right light, her hair would turn a fiery red and with those feisty green eyes, ah, there was no doubt she would have been a fighter. That she'd also been a virgin, he'd been certain, and he'd coveted the aspect of being her first. The desire had nearly driven him mad.

Holly had never seen him like he'd been that night, angry,

horny, and looking for an avenue of release. Instead, she'd been in the wrong place at the right moment and he'd taken a frightened, helpless girl down a dark path of no return. The fact that she hadn't fought him had angered him further. He'd wanted a full-out brawl with screaming and slapping and pounding. Holly had been frightened; he'd seen the fear in her eyes. When she'd refused to fight back, his adrenaline then, like now, ignited with a fire he couldn't restrain. Yes, it should have been Abby. Abby would never have just lain there and taken it. She would have fought him tooth and nail. He smiled at the thought, feeling the excitement racing through him, waking a part of him that had long been dormant.

A moment later, he remembered the phone call. Sooner or later Abby would talk. Eventually she would tell someone what he'd done and the truth would come out. And when it did, his life would be ruined. He had to put a stop to it. As his mind began to formulate a plan of action, he closed the small spiral notebook and shoved it into the bottom drawer of the kitchen desk beneath a calendar, some expired coupons, and a couple of old phone books. He stood up, readjusted his boxer-shorts, and headed back to bed. His wife couldn't quite satisfy his explosive need but she could definitely take the edge off.

Abby was pouring over an order form when Joyce walked into the office later that afternoon. She heard the approaching footsteps but didn't look up from the column of numbers she was tallying.

"Do you have plans tonight?" Joyce asked, a suspicious inflection resounding in her voice.

With her fingers flying over the keys on the calculator, she replied, "Why?"

"Is there something you want to tell me?"

Abby sighed at the untimely intrusion. "Hang on a sec," she said, "I need to finish this." Adding the three remaining lines of numbers and totaling the figure, she pulled the paper strip from the calculator and jotted the end sum into the correct column on her paperwork. When she looked up, her mother was standing in the doorway, hands on hips, looking horribly impatient. Abby leaned back in the chair and dropped the pen in her hand onto the desktop. Lifting her arms, she pointed both palms upward on either side of her, feigning innocence. "What?" she asked.

"You've been holding out on me." Joyce outright accused her.

"What are you talking about?"

Joyce Warren tried to give her best stern look, but failed miserably as a huge grin broke across her features. "Chad Austin?"

Abby's green eyes flashed wide at the sound of his name. Was it possible that rumors of her evening with Chad had made its way full-circle already? Rumors ran more rampant through a small town than it did an old-fashioned ladies church social.

"Well?"

"Well what?" Abby asked.

Joyce groaned aloud with mock exasperation. Letting her hands fall to her sides, she walked, or a more fitting description might be stomped, farther into the room. Taking what she meant to be an intimidating stance in front of the desk, she asked her question in a more direct fashion. "Do you or don't you have a date tonight?"

An easy smile flirted with Abby's lips. Was her mother in a complete uproar because she had a date, or was it more particularly centered on the fact that she had a date with Chad Austin?

"Abigail? Answer me!" Joyce demanded, her petite body trembling with excitement. Her inquiry was as equally intruding as any BFF's could be. Even the short spikes of her dark hair were quivering.

Abby shook her head with amusement. "How do you know about my date with Chad?"

"Because I just saw him out front," she said. "He asked me to tell you that he would pick you up at six. If it's too early, you're supposed to call him."

"Oh," Abby said, her heart fluttering outrageously within her chest. She couldn't hold back the embarrassing pink flush or the grin that flooded her face. Her worrisome day had been for naught. Chad Austin still wanted to see her. A chill of eager anticipation shot straight up her spine.

"So, it's true. You are going out with him?"

Abby nodded her head as the phone rang.

Joyce Warren met her daughter's brilliant gaze and smiled pleasantly. "Good for you," she said, then turned toward the door. "I'm headed back to the hospital. I'll see you later," she continued as she walked away, leaving Abby alone in the office.

Flustered that her mother was genuinely delighted, Abby chuckled and picked up the receiver. "Warren Lumber."

The same empty connection that had greeted her earlier that morning hung eerily on her end of the receiver. It was the fourth such call today; the last three had been here at the lumberyard. Growing tired of the crank calls, she slammed the handset back into its cradle, hoping the disconnection was loud and annoying on the other end. Sliding her paperwork into a metal bin on the corner of the desktop, Abby stood up and purposefully walked out of the office. She couldn't worry about it now; she had a date she needed to get ready for.

Chapter Eight

ABBY'S EYES FLASHED with excitement as she bit into the loaded quarter-pound cheeseburger in her hands. Chad smiled at her enthusiasm. He'd wanted to take her somewhere other than Macy's Café, somewhere a little nicer, but she'd insisted. The animated groan she gave had him diving into his own burger with gusto. He watched the look of delight cross her features as he chewed and swallowed. "Is it as good as you remember?"

She sighed with contentment. "Better."

The bell above the front door jangled someone's arrival and it drew his attention. Recently retired Bud Carson and his wife Millie strolled in. They were a charming couple, short, grayed, and wrinkled. Their sons, Frank, Doug, and Ben had recently taken the reins of the family heating and cooling business, leaving them more time to spend with their five grandchildren, soon to be seven. Doug and his wife Kelly were expecting twins in November. Chad waved to them, as did the other patrons crowding the small café. The couple returned greetings and shuffled over to the single remaining table in the middle of the restaurant.

Macy's Café was owned by Bruce and Charlotte Brewer. As inheritances go, the café was first opened by Charlotte's grandparents and like many small town businesses, had been passed down from one generation to the next since its grand opening in 1941. It was an old-fashioned restaurant with the original green Formica countertops and backless silver stools that were bolted to the floor. At some point in time the stools had been upgraded with black vinyl seats. An ancient cash register was located at the end of the counter just to the left of the front door. The floor was covered in square dull gray tiles, shined and sealed monthly with a solid coat of wax. There were five booths lining the back wall with the same aged green Formica tabletops. Chad sat across from Abby on the black vinyl seat of the center booth. The middle of the room housed a dozen smaller square tables with four chairs each, spread about the open space, leaving just enough room for one of the two waitresses to squeeze through.

It was definitely a small town gathering place with black-framed newspaper photos and accompanying articles that highlighted the Mills Pond Panthers football and basketball seasons hanging on eggshell-colored walls. His senior year, they had won the state football championship and a huge photo of the entire team hung on the wall behind him between the pinball machines and the restroom facilities. Underneath it, locked in a clear acrylic case, was the winning football signed by the entire team. He smiled as he recalled that triumphant championship game. From the town celebration that ensued, you'd have thought they'd won the Super Bowl.

"Penny for your thoughts," Abby said, pulling his gaze back toward her.

He met her inquiring features and couldn't help broadening the grin that formed across his cheeks.

"What?" she asked, her curiosity clearly piqued.

He leaned toward her, reaching up with his thumb to gently wipe away a large glob of ketchup that clung to a spot just beneath her lower lip. Expecting a reaction rich with embarrassment, he was quite surprised when she caught his hand with her fingers, raised it to her mouth and ran her moist pink tongue across the pad of this thumb where the rescued red condiment had been. He knew he was staring at her with shocked amusement as he willed himself to breathe. Somehow, she'd managed to stop that natural process all together. The minutes following became a blur. All he could think about was the strength in her fingers, the soft feel of her lips and tongue on his skin. If she'd had the nerve to draw his entire thumb into her mouth, he wasn't sure what his next course of action might have been. Though it would have been far from chivalrous on his part, dragging her out of the booth and into the bathroom very well may have been her fate.

Somehow they made it to the truck, though he couldn't remember paying for their dinner. His mind was still swimming with the debilitating effects of her actions as he backed out of their parking space. Gazing at her across the cab, he thrust the gear into drive and the truck lurched forward.

"Thank you for dinner," she said for the third time. Meeting his gaze, she smiled.

"You're welcome."

There was something about the open candidness her smile offered that had always teased his senses. He tried to put a sexy spin on the one he gave in return, hoping it had an equally taunting effect. With Jason Aldean singing something about a big green tractor drifting through the cab from the radio, she pulled her gaze away from his and settled her hands onto her lap, tangling her fingers together. He marveled at her distinct mannerisms—which he recalled with utmost clarity—as he watched her worry her bottom lip between her teeth. The action was causing a strong desire to coil through him. When she turned her face in his direction, he encountered cool liquid aqua. Oblivious of the affect her gaze had on him, he took a deep breath trying his best to gain control. A rush of wayward thoughts bounded through his head, many of them premeditated by more than a decade. "Do you remember Darren Rustin?" he finally asked. "He came over to our table last night."

She nodded her head. "Darren the super jock? He was involved in football, basketball, track, baseball, and even car racing if I can remember correctly."

Chad threw his head back and laughed. "That would be him though the title doesn't fit any longer, except for the car racing. He blew out his knee playing college football. After finishing school, he came back to Mills Pond, married Becky Spencer, and took a job at Sam Montgomery's Hardware store."

"Really? Becky's family owned that big house on First Street."

"The bed and breakfast?"

Abby nodded her head. "That would be the one."

"They still do. Becky works there part time when the kids are in school."

"Oh," she said.

Chad heard the catch in her voice and wondered if Becky had been one of Chase's cronies. He was going to have to figure out who was in that group in order to better protect her. "Darren is hosting a bonfire at his parents' farm tonight. I was hoping you might like to go?"

Abby couldn't squelch the gasp that escaped from her throat. "Are you sure you want *me* to go with you?"

As he gazed at her again, his features sobered and he took on a more serious tone of voice. "Absolutely," he said. "However, I don't want to pressure you or make you feel uncomfortable."

"It's too late for that," Abby said. "This whole town makes me uncomfortable."

Her words sounded sad and Chad reached across the interior with his right hand, clasping both of hers within the firm strength of his grasp. "We're going to fix it. I promise."

She sighed apprehensively. "Right."

"I promise," he repeated firmly. "We don't have far to drive so if you don't want to go, you need to tell me now."

She moved her gaze from their entwined fingers to his face. At that moment, she looked small and fragile. Abby forced a quick gulp of stale air down her throat while a solid shiver shook her body. Closing her eyes, her features softened. When they opened again, she gave him a tenacious smile. "I guess now is as good a time as any to get started, huh?"

His fingers lightly squeezed hers. "It will be okay. I'll be right there with you."

"Chad, why are you wasting your time?"

"Wasting my time?" he asked, certain that his confusion registered across his features as he looked in her direction.

"With me," she whispered.

She met his gaze then and held it. What he saw reflecting back belied her question. The dual aqua pools held such a powerful look of hope it made his chest ache. "Abby," he said, "I know you don't have any reason to trust me, but I'd hate to see you walk away before giving me a chance to prove myself."

She dropped her face toward her lap; he suspected it was a ploy to hide her expression from him. Sliding her left hand from beneath his, she placed it on top. "You don't have to do this," she said.

He realized at once that she wasn't running, not yet, and a dazzling smile lit up his face. "Oh, yes I do."

She lifted her head abruptly, her eyebrows creased together with reservation she didn't put into words.

"You coming home gave me a second chance and you can bet that cute backside of yours that I'm not going to let the opportunity pass me by again," he said. Though he missed her facial reaction to his words, he knew she was watching him as he maneuvered his blue Silverado off the gravel road and through the open gate of a huge pasture. The truck burrowed through the bumpy terrain of the massive field, sending them bouncing up and down in the bucket seats. There were several vehicles, mainly trucks, parked in front of them.

He pulled up alongside an older model Jeep with its top removed and hit the brake. "Here we are," he said.

Abby rolled her eyes in response. "Great, can we go now?"

He chuckled as he shut off the truck and released his seatbelt. "Stay put," he said, opening his door. "I'll help you down."

"Guess that's a no," she said when he appeared in front of her with the door ajar.

Chad smiled and shook his head, then slid his palm across her lap to loosen her seatbelt. Her eyes were wide with apprehension as he gazed into them. His breath caught in his throat when he lifted his hand, trailing an index finger down the soft curve of her jaw. He was hoping that his easy caress would offer support but what he got was something he hadn't expected—a full electric charge. They looked at one another and stopped breathing altogether.

Abby blinked but no words came as she moved forward, away from the seat. His hands hastily caught her waist and she was against him, or he was against her. Their bodies were touching from chest to stomach, his hands imprinting upon her hips as he pulled her from the cab. He slid her down the length of his body, feeling the heat of her skin blazing through her jeans. Chad blew out a quick breath when her feet landed squarely on the ground. His voice was strained when he finally spoke. "Ready?" he asked.

Biting her bottom lip, she nodded her head and he slipped his arm around her shoulders, pulling her close. She gave him one last timid look and took a step forward. Her strides were determined ones as they walked across the crunchy, choppy dead leftovers of harvested crop. When they reached the edge of the gathering, she looked dazed and he could feel her fear suspended just beneath the surface. "Abby?"

Her eyes followed his voice as she turned to look at him. She even tried to smile.

He touched her cheek with his palm. "Are you okay?"

A solid pink flushed across her skin. "I'm fine."

"Hey, you made it!" Darren Rustin greeted. He pointed as he passed by with two large bags of ice thrown over his shoulder. "Beer's in the back of the truck and there are hotdogs with all the fixings, chips, and marshmallows by the coolers on the other side of the bonfire. Help yourselves."

"Thanks," Chad said, turning his body to face her as Darren walked away with his icy haul.

Abby gave him another nervous smile.

"Are you sure you're okay?"

"Yes, I'm fine."

"All right," he said, reaching for her hand and threading his fingers through hers as he led them toward the black Ford F150 and a cold beverage. Pulling two bottles from one of several available coolers, he let go of her hand and twisted the cap off the first bottle of beer, handing it to her.

"Thanks," she said.

He opened the second bottle and clanked it against hers.

With the burst of orange and pink against the backdrop of deepening blue came the long shadows of twilight as they settled over the field. During the next hour while darkness descended, they stood just outside the ring of heat the bonfire put off and he introduced or reintroduced her to the gathering crowd of townsfolk. Karl Dunkin, the owner of Karl's Gas & Tow. Bobby Dell, whom she knew as a machinist from the lumberyard, and Rudy Anson who'd graduated from the same class as she and Chase. He worked for his father's tractor company, Anson Implements. And there was Caleb West who worked with Darren at Montgomery Hardware, with his girlfriend Amy, among others.

Chad kept Abby close, observing her body language for signs of unease. Every time her beer got low, someone handed her another. After a quick look to confirm the direction of her gaze, he studied her as she watched Caleb and Amy roasting hotdogs in the leaping flames of the huge bonfire. Several large logs were piled at least three feet high and blazed with an array of colors ranging from bright yellow to deep red. He was fascinated as they played shadow against light over the curves of her profile. A thick burnt hickory smell permeated the air while smoke drifted slowly skyward as it separated from the flickering blaze.

She looked up at him, her eyes brightly reflecting the glinting fire and he smiled. When she returned it, he crooked his index finger a couple of times, directing her to follow him. As he turned away and lowered his arm, he felt her palm slide against his as she stepped up beside him. He led her toward the coolers and located an open package of marshmallows. There were several wooden sticks lined up against a small white plastic folding table and he grabbed one, loading two large pliable white puffs onto it before handing it to her. "Here you go," he said, smiling as she looked at his offering with casual disinterest. "Don't tell me you don't like marshmallows?"

"What if I don't?"

"Well, that's just plain un-American."

With a shake of her head, she grabbed the stick from him and turned away. Walking toward the fiery blaze, she jabbed the loaded end into the dancing orange flames. By the time he had a second stick loaded with dual marshmallows; Abby's roasting attempt had caught fire.

"See," she said, thrusting the raging inferno in his direction.

Laughing, Chad grabbed the stick from her, blew out the fire, and pulled the charcoaled goo off the end, popping it into her mouth. She giggled, then chewed and swallowed the burned lump of sugar.

"That wasn't so bad, was it?" he asked.

Smacking her sticky lips together, she lightly shook her head. "No."

His gaze moved from her shimmering eyes toward her mouth and he smiled. "Hold still," he said, reaching his thumb toward the corner of her mouth where a thin string of white marshmallow goo had taken up residence. With the gentlest of touches, he wiped it away.

She groaned. "Twice in one night! You must think I'm a sloppy eater."

Dang if she wasn't cute when she was embarrassed. "Not at all. I'm just taking advantage of the opportunities it presents."

"Opportunities?" she asked, doing her best not to laugh.

He took a step closer to her, his gaze burrowing into hers. It took all the control he had to keep his face from breaking into a full grin. "You want to find something else to eat?"

She graced him with a brilliant smile. "Only if you have a pack of Wet Wipes in that truck of yours."

"I might. Maybe we should go look?" Chad suggested in a flirting fashion. When a smile born of temptation crossed her face, he laughed out loud. "Come on," he said, dropping the marshmallow loaded stick and grabbing her hand with all the eagerness of a teenager on his dream date. Turning away from the bonfire, their speedy escape was cut short as they nearly smacked into Chase Austin's rigid form as he blocked their path. He stood mere inches from them, glaring angrily.

"Hey," Chad said, trying to keep his tone light. "I didn't know you were here."

Chase crossed his arms over his chest. "I'd say you're a little distracted."

Chad didn't like the intimidating stance or the sharp edge of Chase's voice. Not wanting Abby to be the recipient of his brother's continued rage, he stepped in front of her.

"Why is *she* here?" Chase demanded.

"I invited her."

"She doesn't belong here."

Chad turned his torso in order to gauge Abby's angst. Her eyes flared wide with trepidation and he caught her elbow with his hand. "It's okay," he said, his voice filled with gentle support. Turning his attention back toward his brother, he glared menacingly. "Who made you judge and jury?"

Chase leaned to the left so he could view Abby directly. "She's only looking to gain a sympathetic ear. And who better to get it from than my own brother?"

Chad moved his body back between them, blocking the ugly, intimidating stare Chase was aiming in Abby's direction. "Look Chase, I pursued Abby, not the other way around."

"Why?"

"That's my business, little brother."

"She killed Holly."

"I know you believe that," Chad said as he took a step closer, bending forward so that Chase could clearly decipher his features. "But it was an accident. Abby was just as much a victim as Holly was."

Chase nearly barked. "The hell she is."

Chad backed up a step, carefully analyzing the hard angles of Chase's features. With the flickering fire in front of him, his brother's familiar eyes glinted, reflecting the sputtering orange glow from the fire, giving off the impression of a sinister stranger. His jaw was clenched so tightly it looked as though his teeth may shatter. The two men glared at each other, their brotherly ties forgotten in the heat of the moment, the glittering liquid amber color of their eyes fiercely burning into one another.

"Maybe we should go," Abby said, tugging the back of Chad's black T-shirt.

"She's a smart girl." Chase growled. "You should listen to her."

Chad turned his face toward hers. "You have as much right to be here as anyone else."

Chase chuckled, not amused. "Not really."

"This is her town too, Chase. Her family and her friends are here."

Chase swept his arms out wide. "Look around, Chad. Do you see any of *her* friends here?"

Abby's features fell flat as Chase's words sunk in. The joy and freedom they'd enjoyed only moments ago had fully disintegrated. Chad didn't know whether to wrap her in his arms or knock his brother out. He wanted her to fit in and knew that with his help she would. But it wouldn't happen tonight. Their bittersweet moment had been ruined. And with the free flow of alcohol, it would only get worse the longer they stuck around. He watched helplessly as she set her beer bottle on the ground and fled toward the truck without saying a word. His eyes followed her path while her stride quickly took her in the opposite direction. When he turned back toward Chase, all he wanted to do was punch the smug smile off his brother's cocky features.

———◦《◦》◦———

When he saw Abby he'd nearly choked on the mouthful of hot-dog he'd just shoveled in. What kind of magic had she weaved? Chad looked like a doped-up puppy following her around with his tail wagging as he introduced her to everyone. He slammed down the remnants of the beer he was tightly gripping. Looking at the empty bottle, he realized the sudden desire to smash it and drag a broken shard of glass across that slim, ivory throat of hers. That should do the trick. If she bled to death she couldn't talk. The thought made him smile. Of course, he would take his time and do all those things he longed to do first. He'd hoped the early morning encounter with his wife would quench his need but it hadn't even come close. He must have gotten a little too rough because she'd called him an animal and crawled out of bed before they'd finished.

He swore under his breath. It would be easy for Abby Warren to destroy everything he'd worked hard to keep at bay. Prank phone calls and bad-mouthing her was evidently not enough. She wasn't afraid. Not yet. But she would be—soon. His main concern was whether Chad would become a problem as well. He certainly hoped not, but in the end it didn't matter. He would do whatever he felt necessary to stop the threat of exposure.

Chapter Nine

ABBY WANDERED THROUGH the dark stumbling across the uneven ground. She'd known in her gut it was a mistake to come, but she'd been selfish in wanting to spend time with Chad. She loved the way she felt when he was near her—all warm and tingly. She would need to analyze the reasons behind those feelings when she got home. Right now, though she was putting distance between them, she could feel his presence clear across the field.

Stopping to catch her breath, she heard footsteps still at a distance and turned to face the dim shadows behind her. Unable to pinpoint a shape or outline of any kind, the fine hairs on her arms stood on end. Panic churned as adrenaline pooled. She whipped around and continued toward the truck. She was closer to it than the exuberant crowd hanging near the bonfire. Besides, she wasn't about to trace her steps backward and risk running into whoever it was following her. Squelching the cry that tried to tear from her throat, she started to run. The rutted terrain made it difficult to traverse as she tripped over a mound here or fell into a pothole there. The line of vehicles was close. The stalker was closer. She wasn't going to make it.

"Abby!"

Her heart was pounding within her chest a staccato of beats that she was sure would be noticeable in broad daylight. The sound of her name rang in her ears. Though the voice it had come from was muffled and breathless, it was still familiar. She drew to a stop and spun toward it. "Chad?"

Within a few steps, he was standing in front of her. "I'm so sorry," he said. "I didn't mean to scare you."

She placed one hand against her aching side and the other over her mouth to stifle her gasp. The cool sheen of sweat that had broken across her skin sent a chill through her in the heated summer darkness. Her throat was dry and she couldn't seem to find the words she wanted. Standing in front of his stilled form, the light from the bonfire melded with the inky blackness surrounding them, making only his silhouette visible. The way his shoulders lifted and fell, she was sure he was fighting to catch his breath.

After a moment of silence, his hand reached for the crooked elbow resting above her hip. When his hand slid against her skin, his fingers wrapped around her arm and he lightly turned her in the direction she'd originally been headed. "Come on," he said.

She went willingly. He led them around the front line of parked vehicles, putting more distance between them and his brother with every step they took. Finally, the dark outline of the truck came into view and he escorted her around to the passenger side. After opening the door, the light momentarily blinded them and she blinked rapidly, trying to adjust her vision.

"I'm sorry," he said for the second time as he helped her climb into the truck.

Now that Abby was seated inside the cab, she was eye level with him. Leaning toward him left only a couple of inches between his face and hers. "Knock it off," she said now that she had her voice back. "It's not your fault."

He hung his head, hiding whatever emotion was flickering within his gaze. His hair, darker than it should be in the defused light, stuck out at odd angles on the top of his head. "I should never have brought you here."

It was her turn to play champion. Reaching out her hand to lightly caress his jaw with her fingertips, she felt the clenched bone beneath her touch. "Actually, I'm glad that you did."

His head lifted instantly, his glittering eyes boring into hers. "Seriously?" he asked.

She focused on his skeptical tone and dropped her hand, settling it on her lap. The look of awe etched across his features was endearing and she couldn't hold back the smile that tugged at the corners of her mouth. She nodded. "Yes. Not everyone here tonight was cruel or even unfriendly. Besides that, I got to spend more time with you." It was more information than she'd intended to give but she felt assured he would appreciate the acknowledgement.

He gave her a wistful look. "You know," he said, his voice soft and hesitant, "I never even asked how you might feel about me. When I heard you were coming back to town, the only thing I could concentrate on was seeing you again. I walked out of your life once without telling you how I felt and I wasn't going to repeat that mistake. Instead, I've been dragging you all over the place just assuming you reciprocated those feelings. So I'm wondering now, albeit a little late, how you really feel about all of this?"

She sat for a moment, enjoying his pensive manner, letting his words flow over her as she digested them. Closing her eyes, she let a heavy emotional flood surge through her. When she spoke, her voice was barely a whisper. "Without a doubt, I can assure you that those feelings have been mutual for a long time now."

As though her words had turned a rusty spigot wide open, his hands were on her waist, her body turning toward his with no effort of her own. His palms slid down her legs, catching behind her calves, pulling her forward on the seat. Her legs automatically spread apart to accommodate the width of his body between them.

Gazing at him, her lips half-parted with surprise and she had only a split-second to realize that this was the moment she'd dreamed of for most of her life. It was the moment that haunted her late at night when she lie alone in bed, sheets twisted awkwardly around her body. Her mind filled with images that left her consumed with a hunger she couldn't satisfy, nor believe she even deserved. His mouth was upon hers then, not soft and tentative as she'd always envisioned, but bold and confident. It distracted her, shoving any thought of another time or place far from her consciousness. She became lost in the moment as he molded his lips to hers, his fingers slipped through her hair moving to grasp the back of her head between his palms.

Abby closed her eyes, giving herself over to the astonishing physical sensations he was creating. She rejoiced in the pliant feel of his lips against hers as his mouth moved across them with urgency she was eager to match. The pressure of his mouth pressed her head back against his hands as he held her in place. A deep, velvety groan crashed through her brain when she wrapped her arms around his trunk and pulled him more tightly against her. Chad's hands trailed down her back, holding her more forcefully to him.

Her breath came in shallow gasps as his delving tongue circled the circumference of her lips. When he explored further, she was thankful her nails were short and blunt as they dug into his cloth-covered back. She gifted him with a low, yet insistent moan that earned her ardent favor as his hands moved down her body, slipping between her and the seat as he cupped the cheeks of her butt with his palms. When he lifted her, she wrapped her legs tightly around his waist. Heat swirled around them as they lost themselves in one another beneath the sallow glow that burned from the dome light attached to the roof of the cab. The passion igniting between them was more than she'd hoped for. It was more than she'd ever experienced and suddenly she never wanted to let him go.

She gasped as he pulled her out of the truck, one arm wrapped around her waist, the other protecting her head as he shifted her through the door frame. To keep from falling, she locked her ankles behind him and bound her arms around his shoulders. Once her body had cleared the potential metal hazard of the doorway, he turned, forcing his back against the side of the truck. She had to unfasten her ankles and he bent his legs to cradle her, keeping her from falling. Letting loose of her head, he trailed wandering fingers down the middle of her back.

Abby was having great difficulty catching her breath as she pressed her mouth against his. Her head was swimming with a multitude of sensations that were jumbled together in messy confusion. While their dancing tongues flirted shamelessly, his hands slid farther down her body. His palms felt like they were burning through the seat of her jeans as he pressed her more snugly against him. An agitated sigh rushed past her lips mingling with his subtle groan, merging devastated need and erupting passion in a forceful, yet sublime way.

Chad leaned his head back against the hard metal behind him and closed his eyes. His chest heaved violently as he fought for breath. She smiled and moved her mouth to his jaw, trailing the tip of her tongue along the edge before sliding down to the thick column of his neck. His whole body stiffened in response to her intimate teasing.

After drawing in a harsh breath, he finally broke the silence. His voice was deep and gravelly as he spoke. "Well, this wasn't such a smart idea."

Abby chuckled, a low throaty sound that didn't help their current predicament. She knew he was referring to the field they were parked in and not their current physical state. Had their desire ambushed them somewhere more private, she wasn't sure either of them would have been able to stop. Her eyes met his and she nodded her head, hoping the joy she saw reflecting in his gaze was exactly what he saw in hers.

———⸺》《《◊》》《⸻———

Chad's adrenaline raced as they drove away from the bonfire. What had transpired between them played over and over in his head as the dark gravel road flew by just outside the open window. He'd hated having to untangle the intimate position they'd managed, but he felt they were being spied upon. He hadn't heard anyone; it was more that he sensed an unwelcome presence hiding in the darkness. It was an eerie sensation, one he hadn't wanted to share for fear of frightening her. The regret that had emanated from her gaze the moment he released her would never be forgotten. Abby had been as frustrated as he at having their spontaneous undertaking cut short, but the last thing he wanted was a witness. She'd been through enough. Even so, he fought to hide the smile that was nearly bursting out of him. "You okay?" he asked, giving her a quick glance from across the cab.

She nodded, turning her head toward him. "You keep asking me that."

His jaw pulled taut and he met her gaze once again. "I just want to make sure I didn't do anything stupid back there."

She smiled a dazzling smile leaving no way to misinterpret her reaction to his surprise ambush. "You didn't."

It was obvious that she'd wanted to kiss him as badly as he'd wanted to kiss her. "That wasn't premeditated," he said, trying to assure her that though he'd had a momentary lapse in judgment, he hadn't meant to take advantage of the situation.

Abby laughed pleasantly. "I haven't accused you of anything."

His head snapped back to look at her again. "You're really not upset?"

Abby gasped. "Are you kidding? I've waited a lifetime to confirm my suspicions."

He finally let out the breath he'd been holding, allowing him to loosen the tense strain in his shoulders. It was one thing to interpret her reaction, but quite another to have his interpretation validated aloud. The smile that flashed across his face was brilliant. "And are they confirmed?"

The smile that encompassed her entire face became one more radiant than he'd ever seen. "Do you really have to ask?"

He was enjoying their banter and wanted to hear more of what might be churning around in her head. "Humor me."

She groaned in a teasing manner. "In my opinion, I think we should have tried that a long time ago."

He couldn't help but laugh. It was an astounding moment between them. The disclosure of their long-shared attraction combined with the intensity of her honesty was something that struck deeply within his chest. She was used to living in a bubble that protected her from the outside world, not trusting anyone enough to let them in. And here she was, sweeping all of her demons aside for him. Her strength and courage filled him with mind-numbing hope. This time around, somehow, he was going to convince her to stay.

They drove silently through town, the truck's bright headlights leading the way. Sneaking peeks at her, Chad was certain she was steadily watching him through her peripheral vision. He found her newfound coyness comforting and smiled.

"What?" she asked.

Busted. He wasn't an adolescent male hiding behind the fear of rejection any longer. He was just man who'd made mistakes, the worst of which was keeping his silence. No longer afraid, he was ready to fight to keep her in his life. He'd completely lost himself in her only moments ago and though it hadn't been the ideal situation, he'd found it difficult to stop. "I wish I knew back then, what I know now."

Abby looked at him, her brow creased while the corners of her mouth pulled slightly upward. "And what would that be?"

He smiled, striving for that sexy angle once again. "I was an idiot showing up in art class every day never having the guts to confess my true intentions."

She laughed in response. "If we're making true confessions here, then I'll admit that there was a lot of mutual idiocy going on back then."

It was his turn to laugh again. Her driveway came up quickly on the right and he pulled the truck into the empty space behind her mother's car, the lights sweeping in a wide arc across the dark lawn. "What the?" he said, throwing the gear into park before the truck had come to a complete stop. Abby lunged forward in her seat before she was yanked backward by the seatbelt. He knew he should apologize for the abrupt action but before the words formed, he pulled on the door handle, shoved his seatbelt aside, and jumped to the ground leaving the door wide open behind him.

"What is it?" she asked as he moved away from the truck.

Though he heard the question, he kept moving, walking around both of her parents' vehicles, coming to a halt behind her car which was parked under the weeping willow at the far left edge of the gravel driveway. His stance grew rigid while his hands collapsed into tightly wound fists. In bold, capital letters the word L-E-A-V-E was sprawled in black spray paint across the rear window of her car. Viewing it caused a sharp, ugly pain to slam into his gut.

"Chad?" Abby asked, walking up beside him and resting her hand against the small of his back. Though he felt the heat of her touch, it was her abrupt gasp that fully caught his attention.

When he looked down and saw the shocked bewilderment cross her features, he reached for her, bringing her body up tightly against his as he wrapped his arms around her protectively. His jaw tightened and his mouth formed a straight line across his face. "Who would do this?" he asked. It was a question aimed at him rather than something he meant for her to answer.

Her response was an uncontrollable shudder.

Chad pulled his gaze away from the offensive demand to look down at her. Her dark hair lay in tangled waves over her shoulders. Her skin was pale in the blanched lamplight and her chin was quivering. She met his gaze with an unblinking stare. Her voice was a stiff, cold whisper. "He's still here," she said.

Wrenching her against him, he caressed her neck with his fingertips. "It's okay. I won't let anything happen to you."

When her whole body began to tremble, he swore under his breath and crushed her to him, tighter than before. She seemed so small and fragile. Her head fit perfectly into the hollow between his neck and shoulder and he stroked her hair with his fingers. Unbelievably, the soft scent of honeysuckle assaulted his nostrils and he silently cursed himself for allowing her smell to outrageously flirt with his senses at such an inappropriate time. God help him, he wanted to kiss her again—kiss away her fear of the past and assure her a peaceful future. But how could he do that when someone actually wanted to scare her? He quickly realized that someone in this town, someone he knew personally, was a rapist and a murderer. And the fact that his attention was now focused on Abby nearly made Chad sick to his stomach.

As he stroked his hand down her back, her fists balled tightly into the material of his T-shirt on either side of his waist. She pulled away slightly, peering up at him. From the light of the streetlamp two houses down, he could see fear and anguish wash across her creamy complexion. Her voice was barely audible when she spoke. "The calls."

"What?" he said, lifting her chin with the pad of his thumb.

She swallowed hard. "The calls," she said, just slightly louder.

"Abby, what calls?" he demanded. Chad knew his voice was gruff, certainly more than he'd wanted, but his touch was incredibly gentle as he coaxed the desired information out of her.

She closed her eyes for a brief second. Unshed tears glittered in her gaze when she opened them. She sighed and drew in a deep breath before continuing. "I thought the phone calls I got today were just prank calls from kids with too much time on their hands."

His fingers brushed against her cheeks as he held her face between his palms. He couldn't quiet the panic racing through him. "Honey," he said softly, "what did the caller say?"

Her eyes met his and held but she only blinked in response.

"Abby?"

She took a slow, deep breath. "I should never have come back," she said.

Anger shot through him that she could so casually cast him aside. He spread his fingers wide to encompass more of her face and gave her *the death stare*. It had always worked with Chase, much like a power play, getting him to give in or give up information. He was hoping for the same effect now. "Don't," he said. "It's too late to run. You're here. We're involved. You're innocent and we are going to get to the bottom of this."

She returned his gaze briefly and closed her eyes, breaking contact. Finally, she answered him. "There was no one there Chad, just dead air."

"They started today?"

Abby tried to nod her head but he wouldn't let go of his hold on her. "Yes. The first one was this morning before I got out of bed. There were three more at the lumberyard."

"Whoever it was didn't say anything?"

"No. But they stayed on the line for a few seconds each time."

Chad let a deep, irritated groan bubble up his throat. He abruptly slid his hands down her back as he tried to push the anger aside.

"What do you think?" Abby asked.

"I think we need to talk to your mother and then call the police."

She wrapped her arms around his middle and leaned into him. He held her there for a few moments longer. Finally, he stepped back and took her hand. Together, they turned away from the vandalized car and walked toward the house.

Chapter Ten

IT ENDED UP being a late night. After Abby had gotten her mother out of bed, Chad insisted they call the police. Deputy Gary Nelson was dispatched to the house around midnight. The three of them stood on the porch and watched the officer climb out of his black and white cruiser. Though she'd never met him, he was wearing the same dull uniform of brown trousers and matching button-down shirt she remembered from her youth. The shade of his shortly cropped hair was lost in the dark, as was the color of his eyes. He had a medium, athletic build and a comforting demeanor. He admitted moving to Mills Pond sometime after Abby had left and she was thankful for that small detail as it made him detached, yet professional.

Deputy Nelson had inspected her car, taken photographs, and made notes for his report. He interviewed the neighbors whose curiosity had caused them to stumble onto their lawns while he was analyzing the crime scene. Unfortunately, no one had seen a thing. Several houses around them remained dark but the deputy assured they would be followed-up with the next morning. Even so, Abby remained skeptical and didn't maintain much optimism for an eyewitness. It was obvious the offender had been careful not to leave incriminating evidence behind.

After the deputy left, Abby poured a steaming cup of coffee from the fresh pot her mother had made and wearily shuffled toward the table. There was something floating at the edge of her consciousness that her brain was not quite ready to digest and it left her feeling awkward and uptight. With the gazes of both Chad and her mother upon her, she pulled out the empty chair between them and sat down.

Shoving the messy bangs of her dark hair out of her eyes, Joyce spoke up. "Why didn't you tell me about the phone calls?"

Beneath the tabletop, Chad slid his palm against hers, entwining their fingers together in silent support. Abby took a deep breath before speaking. "Honestly, I found them severely irritating but never considered it a problem. School is out for the summer. I just assumed they were from some kid seeking a break from boredom."

"Do you seriously think this has anything to do with an accident that happened ten years ago?" Joyce asked.

Chad squeezed Abby's hand and leaned forward in his chair. "It's the only reasonable explanation. Phone calls are one thing; why else would someone tell Abby to leave?"

Joyce continued. "You're sure it's not a stunt played by some jealous woman to get your attention?"

Chuckling quietly in an effort to lighten the mood, Chad responded. "Though that sounds preferable to the situation at hand, I can assure you it's not the case."

Joyce groaned and lifted her hand to her forehead, kneading out the tension with her fingertips. "I just can't believe this. How could someone hold a grudge for that long?"

Abby shrugged her shoulders. "I had a really bad feeling about coming back," she said. "I'm sorry."

Chad leaned toward her touching his shoulder to hers. "It's not your fault, Abby," he said.

Joyce nodded her head in agreement. "Do you think Chase could have anything to do with this?"

Abby watched Chad's jaw tighten ever so slightly.

"No," he said with an adamant tone to his voice.

The conversation was not taking a direction Abby had expected. Well, she wasn't exactly sure what she'd expected, but she wouldn't let accusations fly with no way to confirm them. "I don't see how he could. He was at the bonfire tonight," she said.

"But he lives just a block down the street." Joyce's gaze moved to focus on Chad. "And he can't be very happy that you've been spending time with Abby."

"Oh, he's not," Chad said, rubbing his chin distractedly. He then focused his gaze on Abby. "But then again," he continued, turning his attention back toward her mother, "he knows he has no say in my romantic life."

Joyce sighed wearily. "Well, nothing is going to be solved tonight," she said, pulling herself up from her chair. Picking up the half-filled cup of coffee, she carried it to the sink and poured the still steaming brew down the drain. Setting the cup in the basin, she looked up. "I wish your dad was here."

"He'll be home soon," Abby said, though the thought didn't help her feel any better about the situation.

Joyce nodded her head. "Not soon enough." With sadness displayed across her features, she gazed at Abby. Her voice was soft and perhaps a bit wary when she spoke. "You know your dad loves you, right?" she asked.

Abby looked away, focusing instead on the tabletop. Chad squeezed her hand once again and she felt his support rocket through her entire being.

"Abby, you have to understand that your father is a proud man, a pillar of the community."

"Oh, I know that, Mom. He made his disappointment quite clear."

"Disappointment?" her mother repeated. "Abby, when the

townspeople began pointing fingers towards you, he stood his ground and defended your innocence."

Shocked by her mother's words, Abby lifted her head to view her mother's face as she spoke. "I couldn't leave the house because the ridicule from my so-called friends was downright malicious and I couldn't stay inside because I didn't know how to face Dad's indignation. The silent treatment hurt worse than anything else. Pooled together, the situation was simply too overwhelming. Right or wrong, I did the only thing that made sense at the time. I ran as far and as fast as I could."

"Oh, Abigail," Joyce cried, "your father was upset because he couldn't control the situation. He didn't know how to protect his only child from such a horrible circumstance. He was frustrated and sad because you felt that leaving was your only option. At the time, he didn't know what to do. You were so miserable that he felt it best just to let you go."

Tears welled in Abby's eyes. "He believed I was innocent?"

"Of course he did," Joyce said. "He—we never once doubted you for a single moment."

Abby closed her eyes and took a deep breath. She'd been wrong all these years. Because of the ongoing silence—for which she was equally responsible—she'd allowed herself to believe her father had been so disillusioned with what he thought she'd done that he'd disowned her. With the truth sinking in, her body began to tremble with relief. Chad quickly loosened his grip on her hand and slid his arm around her.

"Your father loves you, Abby," Joyce said, taking a step toward her and placing a warm hand upon her shoulder.

Abby nodded her head and put her hand over the top of her mother's. "Maybe it's time to make amends and put an end to the silence," she said.

Her mother agreed. "I think that's a great idea."

"Tomorrow," Abby whispered and was gifted with a pleasant smile followed by a large yawn which her mother tried to hide behind her palm.

Lightly squeezing Abby's shoulder before letting go, her mother turned toward the hallway. "It's been a long day. I'm going to try to get some sleep."

"I'll be up in a minute," Abby said.

Joyce glanced back at the pair. "Good night."

"Good night," Chad returned, following her with his gaze as she moved through the door.

Joyce turned back before completely disappearing from view. "Thank you Chad, for protecting my daughter."

He nodded his head and watched her vacate the room, then turned his attention toward Abby and smiled. "It's my pleasure."

With his gaze blazing into hers, Abby could feel the heat coming from his body. On top of everything that had transpired over the past couple of hours, she couldn't believe he could still entice her. A smile of her own flirted with her lips as she focused her attention upon the handsome man sitting next to her. She reached out her palm to caress her fingers over the chiseled line of his jaw. "Yes, thank you."

"Abby," he said, his voice sober, "we have to figure out who was on that road with you."

"How do we do that?"

"By staying alert and keeping our eyes and ears open."

"Chad, no one saw anything. And when no one came forward to corroborate my story, half of this town wanted to put me in jail."

He leaned forward, catching her face between his palms. "But they didn't because you were never guilty of a crime. Whoever is responsible has been visibly shaken by your return. It's obvious he's running scared and that means he'll make a mistake."

"How can you be so sure? He walked into the front yard tonight as if invisible."

"By doing that he's garnered a lot of attention toward himself, and not the kind he wants," he said.

She pulled back from his hands and sat thinking about what her mother had said. "I don't understand why he would he choose to expose himself now. He's gotten away with hiding the truth for years. How can I be a threat to him after all this time?"

Chad cocked an eyebrow. "My theory?" he asked.

Abby nodded her head in response.

"He isn't certain that you don't know who he is. If you know his identity and decide to tell someone, his past comes crashing down on him."

The words sunk in heavily. She hadn't thought of that. She'd never considered that he didn't know Holly had kept his identity a secret. She'd gone to the grave with it. Anger mixed with sadness coiled through her. She closed her eyes against the torrential surge of emotion.

"Abby?" Chad said, his warm fingers slowly gliding down her arms. "Look at me."

She opened her eyes and met his gaze squarely.

"We'll take every precaution," he said. "I won't let anything happen to you."

The way he looked at her made her feel invincible. She felt his strength, like invisible steel bands, wrap around her. She knew with every fiber of her being that he would be there for her. That knowledge made it easier to cast off some of her impending fears. Feeling lighter with every breath, she fought the smile that pulled at the corners of her mouth. "Promise?"

The slow, lazy smile he greeted her with was breathtaking. "You can't keep me away."

She reached up to touch her fingertips to his jaw, lightly sliding them down his neck, coming to rest on his shoulder.

At her touch, his eyes slid closed and immediately flicked back open again. "I should let you get some sleep."

"Probably," she agreed.

He smiled again and his eyes changed from dark amber to melting honey brown. She wasn't sure who led and who followed but she found herself sitting on his lap, his muscular legs bent beneath her. His arms enveloped her, drawing her against his chest as he lowered his head. Their lips connected in a burst of dual eagerness. Her head swayed with dizziness as he assaulted her mouth and she leaned back against his arm and willingly let him work his magic.

When he'd stolen all the air from the room, he pulled away and leaned his forehead against hers. Panting hot breaths into her face, he finally groaned, "I need to go before I do something stupid."

She cupped his face between her palms and gave him a teasing smile. "Now why would you go and do something like that?"

He chuckled. She could feel the depth of it rumbling through his chest. "I tend to lose all rational control when I'm around you."

Abby lightly kissed his chin, then his cheek before leaning back. "Glad to know I'm not the only one."

The easy chuckle rumbling through him shook his body and he hugged her. "Babe, I knew I was going to pursue you when you came home, but I never saw this coming. I had no idea we'd have such an incredible reunion."

Abby traced her index finger over his throat where the edge of his black T-shirt met the golden glow of his sun-kissed skin. "That makes two of us."

"Would you think about something?" he asked, his voice taking on a more serious tone.

"Sure," she said, her gaze moving back to his face. She couldn't help but perceive the hope swimming within the amber depths.

"Would you consider moving back to Mills Pond?"

She closed her eyes and took a deep breath. "The jury is out on that right now."

"I realize there's some idiot running around with a secret he'd rather keep silent, but we'll catch him. Besides that, you're about to lose your apartment. The longer you spend here, the less time you'll have to find a suitable replacement." She gazed into his sweet face once again. That she was sitting here with Chad Austin, well actually on his lap, amazed her. Could this be real? Did he truly want her to stay? Letting out a quick rush of air, she answered as best she could. "Let's take one day at a time."

He sighed and gave her a genuine smile. "I can live with that."

At that moment a horrid squall greeted them as Brewtus lumbered into the room. His demeanor patronizing as he gifted them with a solid green-eyed stare before dismissing their presence entirely.

"What is that?" Chad asked with a low chuckle.

Abby laughed. "Chad, meet Brewtus. Brewtus, meet Chad."

"Nice name," he said.

"Don't give me the credit," Abby said as she watched the orange ball of fluff plop himself down in the middle of the kitchen floor and stick one hind leg straight up in the air. "Brewtus is my neighbor's cat. He had a business trip and couldn't find anyone else to keep him."

"So you brought him with you from St. Louis?" he asked, astonishment clearly evident across his features.

"I did," she said. "However in my defense, it was sort of an emergency and I didn't have time to find a replacement cat sitter."

"Hmmm," Chad said, "sorry to hear that. He's got to be a joy to have around."

Abby shrugged her shoulders in response. "Well, I'll admit he is a bit cantankerous."

"He looks downright arrogant to me. It must have been an interesting drive."

Abby giggled. "Oh, it was. I never knew if he was sleeping or getting ready to attack me from the backseat. Thank goodness the drive wasn't long enough for him to seriously consider the latter."

"You are taking him back?" he asked.

With a nod of her head, she assured him. "As soon as possible."

"Good," he said and then smiled down at her. Before she could return the smile, his mouth was covering hers once again and her brain became lost in his overwhelming presence while the soft coaxing of his lips flooded her with that warm, tingly sensation she never wanted to stop.

Chapter Eleven

SATURDAY AFTERNOON ABBY was thankful to have some time alone as she desperately needed to wrap her head around everything that had happened since her return. Chad was spending the afternoon fishing with Chase. He was hoping for a little bonding time with his brother in order to ferret out some useful information on who might be the one responsible for harassing her. She doubted he would be successful. It was because of her that a great divide had developed between the brothers and she was positive Chase would be less than willing to share anything he might know.

The sun was high above the treetops when Abby stepped onto the covered porch, her old sketchbook in hand. She sat down in one of the heavy Adirondack chairs and crossed her legs Indian style. Flipping the sheets of other works over the top of the spiral metal binder, she found a blank page and settled the book on her lap. Staring intently at the blank canvas, she began to trace Chad's features from memory. From the high forehead to the firm line of his jaw, she moved her black charcoal pencil over the pristine white page. Holding the pencil at an angle, she was able to highlight the taut cheekbones, giving them a softer, more intimate edge. Biting her bottom lip between her teeth as she concentrated, she sharpened the almond-shape of his eyes, adding a wave of long lashes across the rim of the lids and graceful sun-bleached brows. Using her thumb, she carefully smudged the charcoal, creating the subtle horizontal line of his nose and the gentle curves of his lips. The shading effect gave the face dimension, almost as though his features were lifting off the page. Still working her magic, she curved, dipped, and shaded the hairline around the face, smiling at his likeness when she finished.

The memory of his fiery kisses burned into her soul. Had he actually asked her to stay or had she only imagined it? So much had transpired over the past twenty-four hours she wasn't sure where the fine line between truth and fiction lay. The fact that someone had vandalized her car frightened her. It proved easy accessibility and paraded her solitary vulnerability in front of the entire town. If someone truly wanted to harm her, it wouldn't be difficult to accomplish. On the other hand, if their only objective was to pressure her into leaving, they were doing a fairly decent job of it.

Deputy Nelson had come back earlier that morning, questioning the neighborhood by daylight. Just as she'd suspected, no one saw or heard a thing. Whoever it was had waltzed into the yard without being seen. She could take the cowardly way out. That would be the easiest way to make it stop. However, she now had two things she hadn't had three days ago, a fresh start with her family and a legitimate chance at a real relationship. Though her family had some issues to work through, they were on a more solid footing than they'd been in years. She'd shared the worst about herself with Chad and he continued to stand beside her. It had been a long time since she'd felt the type of support he was offering and she wasn't about to walk away from it. Leaving might be the easiest solution, but she had never been known for taking the easy way out.

Some might accuse her disappearance ten years ago as childish or immature. She knew better. Leaving her home, her family, and Holly behind had been the hardest thing she'd ever done. The tranquil life she'd known in her youth had been destroyed. Her best friend's life had been ruthlessly stripped away. The tarnished relationship with her father had been grueling and her confidence undermined by the constant ache of guilt and doubt. It was a miracle she'd been able to hold it together well enough to get through college.

Abandoning the idea of going to college in Kansas City—it wasn't as appealing to her without Holly—she'd stumbled across the College of the Ozarks in Branson, Missouri. When she'd left Mills Pond, it felt as though she'd been abandoned. That pain had gone deep and lasted for a long time. The school was her saving grace as it offered a program to those who couldn't afford the tuition. With federal aid, state grants, and a small scholarship in hand, she'd been one of many students employed by the school and had worked her way through, mainly in the art and pottery departments. After four years of diligent focus, she'd received her bachelor's degree with a major in art education and a minor in art history.

Deciding that St. Louis was artsy, eclectic, and far enough away from Mills Pond, she'd found a roommate and rented a loft downtown. Employed by a small gallery a few blocks away, she'd earned enough money to purchase the equipment and supplies for her glassblowing endeavor. She'd taken advanced classes and found the challenge worth the effort. Within six months, her roommate had moved out but she'd found her own unique style and began creating pieces that were interesting. Soon after, she found a shop where she could consign her designs. Within a few months, a local art critic offered to sponsor a legitimate show featuring her pieces. After that, a steady demand for her work continued.

Five years later, she maintained sales in a handful of galleries in the St. Louis area with more income flowing in from her Internet website. She'd kept busy until the economy tanked. Her income steadily began to shrink as the public became more particular about their spending habits. Though she had a decent amount in savings, her rent went up. As the bills poured in, her savings dwindled. A mild panic had set in by the time she met Ruby Hollister, a local artist who was interested in teaming up with a partner to create glass terrariums. Abby would be responsible for providing the glass globs needed to sustain the terrariums. It looked like a great opportunity on paper but they hadn't gotten their physical production off the ground yet. The stress over the new endeavor, the apartment situation, and now the problems she faced after coming home had her stomach churning constantly.

"Is everything okay?" her mother asked, stepping onto the porch with a pitcher of ice-cold lemonade and two glasses.

Abby smiled as she set the tray down on the table between them and settled herself into the opposite chair. "Yes," she said with a nod of her head. "I'm just reflecting on my journey over the past ten years."

Her mother smiled sadly. "It's been a difficult one, hasn't it?"

"In some ways."

Joyce slowly gazed across the yard before turning her full attention to Abby. "I wish I would have been stronger back then. I feel like our decision to let you go was the wrong choice. We really let you down."

Abby shook her head. "It was my decision to leave."

"But you never should have had to make that choice on your own. It was our responsibility as your parents to defend you, no matter what the cost."

"Mom, you did what you could."

"No, I didn't." Joyce leaned back in the chair and pursed her lips together. "You're my daughter, Abigail. I should have protected you. Instead, I let you walk away from us and in doing so, caused a great deal of pain."

"I'm okay." Abby whispered. "We're all human and we've made mistakes. I ran and you let me. It could've been worse."

"I promise that I will make a better effort to visit you in St. Louis. Three times in ten years really isn't much, is it?"

That wasn't quite true. She'd only been in St. Louis for the past six years and her mother had come to Branson a few times. She had also attended her college graduation. Abby tried to force a smile but failed miserably. The tears came then, cascading down her cheeks and over her throat. She knew coming home was going to churn up old painful memories. However, she'd never have guessed a stalker would be the icebreaker.

While sitting next to her mother, they held hands and let tears from years of denial, anguish, and guilt wash over them. The sketchpad flipped off her lap and fell to the ground with a loud thud. The sound grabbed her attention and Abby gazed at her mother. "Can I ask you something?"

"Yes, anything," Joyce said with a sober nod of her head.

"How would you feel if I stayed?"

"What?" Joyce blinked her heavy tear-stained lashes and her voice trembled slightly when she spoke. "Do you really mean that?"

"My lease is up soon and I haven't found an apartment suitable for a studio."

"You want to move home?" There was so much hope in her mother's voice Abby thought the flood of her tears might start all over again.

"It's a possibility. Chad asked me to think about it."

Joyce's voice shot up an octave. "Oh, Abby!" Her smile was luminous as she gazed at her daughter.

"What?" Abby asked, her face suddenly flushing pink within the shade of the covered porch.

"You really do like him, don't you!" It was more of a statement than a question.

Abby couldn't help but chuckle. "Yes, Mom, I like him."

"Good for you," she said, then lifted the pitcher and filled the two awaiting glasses before the cubes of ice could melt entirely. For the next twenty minutes Abby tried to hold her smile at bay while she listened to all the reasons her mother thought Chad Austin was Mills Pond's most eligible bachelor.

⸺⸺◈⸺⸺

Chad thrust his right arm forward forcing the fifteen-pound test line and attached hook to angle from the tip of his fishing pole to the opposite side of the creek, making a solid *plunk* as it hit the water. He sat in a lawn chair on the edge of the creek bank that wound around the south side of his cabin. The afternoon sky was a brilliant blue as far as the eye could see, devoid of clouds, puffy or otherwise. It was a warm day. Beneath the canopy of trees, there wasn't even the slightest hint of a breeze to rattle through the leafy branches shielding him from the bright rays overhead. He flipped up the lid on the drink cooler beside him and reached down deep into the ice to grab a cold bottle of Bud Light from inside.

The stifling day weighed him down, fitting his mood perfectly. He would much rather be spending it with Abby. Instead, he sat there waiting for Chase to show up. They'd exchanged terse words on the phone earlier so Chad wasn't surprised that his brother was taking his sweet time now. It was a measure taken specifically to irritate him, and it was working. But in all honesty, he had to admit that had the tables been turned, he would have done the same. As brothers, they'd had their fair share of disagreements over the years but nothing quite this caliber before. This was different. This was Abby Warren and he was not about to stand back and allow anyone to hurt her, especially his own brother. Chad couldn't explain why she was so important to him after all this time; he just knew that she was.

Absently, he reeled in the line, watching the hook glide just under the water's edge, sparkling as the sun glinted off the silver steel. The rod jerked lightly when the drag loosened and the hook broke the surface. At least part of the worm was still looped at the end of it. After spooling the remaining line, he reached for the beer sitting in the grass next to his chair. Taking a long gulp from the bottle, he let the cool, crisp amber liquid flow over his taste buds and tonsils before sliding down the back of his throat. There was nothing better, well almost nothing, than a cold beer on a hot summer day. Gripping his fishing rod, he arched his arm backward with a quick motion only to have the entire movement stop short in mid-air.

"Damn it, Chad, you're going to blind me," Chase said with annoyance laced through his voice. He'd seized the pole in his right hand in order to avoid disastrous contact.

"Well don't sneak up on me then," Chad barked.

Chase let go of the fishing pole and pointed toward the black Ford pickup parked in the driveway. "I didn't. I slammed the truck door."

Though Chase was a couple of inches shorter than Chad, Chad had to look up from his seated position to meet his gaze. Their physical traits were similar, mahogany colored hair and pecan brown eyes. Those eyes stared back at him, cold as ice. They stood on opposite sides of a deep chasm neither was willing to cross. Chad pulled his gaze away first, not in defeat, but to fasten the hook to his fiberglass rod and lean it against a nearby tree. "Take a load off," he said, motioning with his head toward a second lawn chair he'd set up earlier.

Chase moved stiffly as he rounded the chair and lowered his body into it. He was wearing tan shorts and began slapping at his right calf. "I didn't bring bug spray," he replied. "I didn't know I'd need it."

Chad ignored the sarcasm. "Have a beer."

Chase looked at his brother and then at the cooler that sat on the ground between them. "Peace offering?"

"No. Just being hospitable."

Chase snorted a caustic laugh but reached inside the cooler. Pulling out a cold bottle, he twisted the cap and tossed it back inside before focusing on the opposite creek bank straight ahead. They sat in compatible silence for several minutes, each nursing a cold bottle of beer. Finally Chase broke the tense-filled silence. "There are a lot of women in this town who would give their eye-teeth to go on a date with you. Why are you chasing Abby Warren?"

Chad chuckled, a low baritone sound. "Most of the women in this town are either married or divorced with children."

"It can't be that you don't like kids. You seem to favor your niece just fine."

A picture of three year old Megan Austin with her honey-blonde pigtails and round cherub face floated into Chad's mind. Chase had met her mother, Kate Armstrong, at the University of Oklahoma. They'd married five years ago and settled in Mills Pond. Kate was the assistant principal at the elementary school while Chase was a science teacher and football coach at the high school. They both believed in the power of education. Although Chad suspected that Chase was also in hot pursuit of a state football championship to hang on his belt. He'd always taken it personally that his graduating class had been unsuccessful in achieving back to back championships for the town. Shaking his head to stop the flow of inconsequential information, Chad smiled tightly and replied. "I love Megan," he said. "I'd also like to have a couple kids of my own one of these days."

"Meaning you don't want to help raise someone else's?"

"It sounds bad when you put it that way."

"I realize Abby is single but she really isn't the right person for you to consider playing house with."

Chad tipped his bottle to chug the remaining contents. "And why is that?" he asked, once he'd swallowed the mouthful.

"You don't know who she is. What she's done."

"I think I have a pretty good idea."

Chase abruptly swung his head toward his brother. "You've only heard what she wants you to hear."

Chad returned the heated gaze. "Is that right?"

"Damn it, Chad," Chase groaned. "Whether you want to believe it or not, she's responsible for Holly's death."

A hefty burst of adrenaline shot through Chad's body forcing him out of the chair and into a standing position. Towering over his younger brother, he began to pace beneath the shade of the trees. "No she's not," he said in a calm, articulate manner.

"Just like Megan, Abby has you twisted around her little finger."

Chad snapped his body toward Chase so quickly that Chase nearly fell backward in the chair. Putting his hands on his hips for lack of knowing what else to do with them, his gaze burrowed into his brother's. "You have no idea what that poor girl has been through."

"Yes I do."

"She found herself in a car at the bottom of a ravine with her best friend lying beside her, injured and unresponsive."

"Because she drove them off the freaking road!" Chase exclaimed.

"Someone forced her off that road and killed your girlfriend in the process."

"I don't believe that," Chase responded. "I never have. And neither did the police."

"They never arrested her."

"Because she wasn't drunk."

"Exactly," Chad said. "She didn't have a drop of alcohol in her system."

"Just because she wasn't drinking that night doesn't mean she didn't cause the car to careen off the road."

"Let me ask you this," Chad said, "if the accident was her fault, why would someone make an effort to harass her after all these years?"

"What are you talking about?"

Chad lowered his arms and rolled his shoulders, easing his tense stance. "Abby has been getting prank calls."

"So someone wants her to leave."

"Someone like you?" Chad demanded.

Chase slammed his half-empty bottle down on the cooler top. It bounced off the surface before landing solidly on the white insulated plastic. "I wouldn't waste my time."

"You did ten years ago," Chad said with an accusatory voice.

Chase clinched his jaw and met Chad's direct gaze. "Yeah, I did. So what? No one wanted her here. The whole town knew she was lying then so why would she think anyone would believe her now?"

"You put her and her family in a horrible position."

"For badgering her a little?"

"You did a great job of destroying a young woman's sanctuary."

"I'm not taking the blame for this. If you want to point your finger at someone, focus on her."

"Chase, because of you and your friends, Abby lost everything including her friends and family. She left Mills Pond with nothing but a car and a suitcase. She put herself through college and built a successful career on her own. You caused her excessive grief and pain. In fact, she and her father haven't spoken since she left."

"Why do you keep accusing me?"

"Because none of it should've happened."

"Are you kidding me?" Chase demanded. "Not only had Holly and I been a couple for two years, we were going to college together. Abby took that away from me."

Chad turned away and began to pace back and forth, his brain swimming with the details surrounding Abby's accounting of that fateful night so long ago. Finally he turned back to face his brother. "Holly wasn't planning to go to college in Oklahoma," he said quietly.

"Did you hear that from Abby?"

"You and Holly were fighting that day because she'd told you she wanted to go to a different school."

"What else did Abby have to say?"

"She told me that's why the two of them ended up out at the lake that night. Holly was upset after your argument. She pilfered a bottle of alcohol from her parents bar and ran to the safest person she knew in order to vent her frustration."

Chase closed his eyes and clenched his jaw but said nothing.

"Abby tried to keep a protective watch over the situation. Leaving the drinking to Holly, she knew she could drive them home safely. But something happened that was beyond her control."

Chase smiled sadly and then quickly pursed his lips together to hide it.

Chad met Chase's gaze. "Someone attacked Holly that night," he said.

Chase turned his head to conceal his reaction to the words that were now out in the open.

"That same someone forced Abby and Holly into the ravine," Chad continued as he watched his brother's face. "And instead of banding together as the friends you were supposed to be, you and the group you recruited ridiculed and bullied her until she ran away."

"That's not fair." Chase argued.

"What's not fair?" Chad asked.

"That you automatically take her side. What about me? What about my loss? You're my brother. You're supposed to back me up."

Chad gave into a heavy sigh. "Chase, I understand you were

angry and needed someone to blame. But you placed that blame on the wrong person. You turned all of her friends against her and she's had to live with that pain for years. Abby didn't do what you've accused her of. Someone else in this town is responsible."

Chase's head shot straight up and he locked gazes with his brother. "I don't believe you."

Chad crossed his arms over his chest and arching an eyebrow, stared at his brother. Their conversation was getting worse, not better. "You're not listening to reason," he said.

"You're certainly getting dramatic over a few prank calls." Chase snorted more than laughed. "Come on, Chad. There are a lot of people in this town that do not like Abby Warren. If you want to play Romeo to her Juliet, that's fine with me. But in the end, a tragedy is all that will come of it."

"Chase, someone spray painted *L-E-A-V-E* in capital letters on her windshield last night. That is not something to take lightly."

Chase leaned his head back and quickly met Chad's gaze. "Well don't look at me," he said, throwing his hands into the air. "I was at the bonfire all night."

Chad breathed in a deep breath and moved toward the chair he'd vacated earlier. Sitting down, he settled his elbows onto his jean covered knees and caught his face under the chin as he eased forward. This conversation wasn't getting him anywhere. Chase's wall of defense was impenetrable. He'd forced Abby into the role of enemy long ago. A short conversation, no matter how logical it may be, wasn't going to change anything. It would take time to put a chink in his armor. It was time he didn't have at the moment. For now, he would ask questions he knew he would get no answers to. "Do you know who might have?"

Chase laughed bitterly. "No."

"I don't want to see Abby hurt any more than she already has been."

"Then maybe she should leave," Chase said.

"You don't have any idea as to who might be behind this?"

Chase groaned loudly. "No, I don't."

Chad eyed him skeptically. He wasn't convinced that Chase wasn't somehow involved. He couldn't even rule out the possibility that Chase himself was responsible. "Fine."

"Fine." Chase mimicked as he stood up. Stretching his arms above his head, he continued. "Are you going to keep seeing her?"

"Abby?" Chad asked.

Chase rolled his eyes. "Who else would I be talking about?"

"Yes," Chad said, his voice steeled with determination.

Chase nodded his head and turned his body in the direction of the driveway. "Good luck then."

"Thanks," Chad responded, "I've got her back, even if no one else in this town does."

"Sounds like a long, lonely road to walk."

Chad gave a slow shake of his head and smiled. "Not even close little brother. Not even close."

Chase chuckled lightly as he turned away. Chad watched him stomp across the thick carpet of green grass covering the front yard. He climbed into the truck and within seconds, the engine rumbled to life. Throwing the gearshift into reverse while chrome gleamed from the glinting sun sent rock spewing in all directions from beneath the tires as Chase put the truck in reverse. Instead of turning around and heading straight up the driveway, he backed up, like a rebel, to the end.

Chapter Twelve

ABBY SAT AT the kitchen table playing gin rummy with her mother while waiting for Chad to arrive. He'd phoned earlier to let her know that his mother had asked him to stop by to take care of a couple of things and he was running behind. He promised to come by as soon as he could get away. It was encouraging to her how devoted he was to his family, Chase included. He hadn't yet told her what had transpired during the conversation with his brother that afternoon so she was sitting on pins and needles waiting.

After discarding her latest offering to the pile, she watched her mother study the remaining cards fanned out in her hand. Brewtus picked that moment to lumber into the room, his overstuffed body swaying back and forth with each dainty—was that even possible—step. His orange fur stuck out at various angles and there were dust bunnies clinging to his rounded belly. He glanced her way and gave a scathing wail as he plopped his back half onto the floor and lifted one leg straight into the air. That particular position was beginning to annoy her. A knock on the tabletop drew her attention back to the game at hand. Her mother was out of moves which meant so was she. As she lay her cards down to tally, the phone rang.

Joyce Warren dropped her remaining cards and jumped up from her chair to answer it. Together they'd made a decision that the next crank caller would be gifted with the shrill of her father's stainless steel coach's whistle, a leftover from the softball days of Abby's youth. Her mother had it in hand when she picked up the receiver, but quickly set it down when she connected with the voice on the other end.

Listening to the caller speak, she gave a short pause before responding. "I'll be right there."

The sound of her voice made Abby immediately stop her poor attempt at reassembling the deck and stand up. "What is it?"

Placing the cordless phone back into its cradle, her mother gave her a befuddled look. "That was Ellen Thayer. She's the dispatcher for the police department. They just got a call that someone has broken into the lumberyard. Deputy Nelson is on his way over there now. I'm supposed to meet him."

"*We* will meet him." Abby corrected.

"What about Chad? Won't he be here soon?"

Abby nodded her head, moved toward the pad of paper near the phone, and grabbed the pen beside it. "I'll leave a note on the door."

"I can't understand this," Joyce said as both women rushed toward the car. "We've never had an ounce of trouble before."

Abby found herself at a loss for words. She was certain her past was spilling over onto her parents' lives. It was the only explanation. It had been a full day since the ugly demand had been painted on her windshield and she was still here, undeterred by the threat. She wanted the town to know that she was innocent of any wrongdoing but if the responsible party was going to threaten her parents, to harm them in any way, the price for justice became too high. Wanting badly to flush out the culprit, she'd have to consider their motives and her exoneration in another light. She knew it would be safer for her family if she just gave in. She'd done it before. Leaving now might not be what she ultimately wanted, but she wasn't about to put her family at risk.

They rode in silence the few minutes it took to get to the lumberyard, located just to the east of town square. The police cruiser was parked in front with a bright spot light shining toward the building. Gary Nelson was nowhere to be seen. Joyce pulled her car up beside the cruiser and snapped the gear into park.

Abby had the door open and was moving to climb out of the car when the seatbelt snapped her back into place.

"Wait," Joyce said, gripping her daughter's upper arm.

"We need to know what's going on."

"Let's wait for Gary to come back to his car."

"Mom—"

"Abigail, do not argue with me."

The grip on Abby's arm tightened and she groaned. Before she could quarrel further, a flashlight beam cut through the darkness. Gary Nelson rounded the corner of the building and walked toward them. With anxiousness swimming in the pit of her stomach, Abby met her mother's gaze. Nodding at one another, they released their seatbelts and exited the car.

"Hey Joyce, Abby," he said as he moved closer. "I don't know who saw what, the call was made anonymously. I can't find any damage. Not even a broken window."

Joyce put a palm to her chest. "Are you sure?"

"Pretty sure. If you want to take a look inside, I'll be happy to check it out."

Abby watched her mother nod and heard the rattle of keys through the darkness, more than saw them. She followed as they walked to the building entrance with Deputy Nelson between them. The door was locked tight; Joyce had to use the key to disengage the bolt. Reaching inside, she flipped the switch to activate the lights. The three of them moved through the door and into the bright open space of the warehouse.

"I don't think anyone has been here," Joyce said, moving past the customer service counter toward the office.

Abby stepped out of the way, allowing Deputy Nelson to follow her mother. Everything appeared to be as it was when they'd closed up late yesterday afternoon. The rows were neat, the floors were swept, the counter orderly. The two registers were locked. No one had tampered with them.

"Nothing appears to be amiss," Joyce said as she followed the deputy out of the office and shut the door behind them. "I really don't think anyone has been here."

Gary nodded his head. After turning off the beam of his flashlight, he tucked it back into his waist holster. "That's odd," he said. "Why would someone make a false report?"

"An anonymous false report," Abby added, stepping around the counter to join them. Could it be an honest mistake on someone's part? Everything appeared to be just as they'd left it. Her stomach began to uncoil just a bit. Was she making more out of this than there was? It was dark outside. Maybe someone viewed a shadow or a swaying tree branch and had gotten spooked. Who better to call than an armed defender of the law? She followed the other two out the door, shutting off the lights behind her. Moving to the side, she witnessed her mother slipping the key into the lock and sliding the deadbolt home. The outside lights were on, the same as when they'd arrived, and Abby was certain the shadows could play with someone's vision.

"I'll check back a little later just to make sure everything is clear," Gary said, shuffling his black boots through the dusty gravel of the parking lot.

Joyce smiled a tight smile. "We'd appreciate that."

"You ladies have a nice evening."

Abby moved toward her mother's silver sedan, opening the door and climbing into the passenger seat. She gazed into the side mirror, noting that Gary was carefully watching them. She wasn't sure if he was simply validating their safe departure or if something more sinister was going on. Groaning inwardly, she knew she couldn't go down that path or soon she'd be suspecting the entire town was out to get her and her family. That was neither healthy nor helpful.

She pulled her gaze away from his reflection to view her mother settling into her seat. "Are you okay?" Joyce asked.

Abby nodded her head in answer.

The key turned in the ignition, firing the engine. Backing up, her mother turned the car toward the street. "Let's go home," she said.

He watched as the three of them came out of the warehouse together. It was obvious they'd found nothing suspicious, except perhaps, his phone call to the police station. He had nothing against Abigail's parents, Paul and Joyce Warren. They were good people. His problem was with her. He didn't want her spreading words of innocence. She was innocent. He was the guilty party. One minute he and his buddies had been drinking and horsing round, the next, he'd attacked Holly Miles simply because he could. She had looked at him with huge tear-filled eyes but she'd smiled at him anyway. He'd never been certain as to what had possessed him, but he'd ignored her tears. Something ugly had taken control and without a fight, he'd given into it. Shamefully, he couldn't even remember the attack. The moment he'd been convinced that she'd stopped breathing was a different story. He recalled that single moment of his past with crystal clarity. Panicked, he'd shoved her beneath the underbrush not far from the parking lot and walked away. He'd been both shaky and queasy but wanted to be sure he could find her body later to dispose of properly.

The next thing he knew, Abby had her arms wrapped around

Holly as they stumbled toward the car. Thoroughly startled, he'd thrown a half empty bottle of Jack Daniels to the ground, ignoring the complaints from his friends as he sprinted to his truck. The red tail lights glaring in front of him as he fishtailed onto the dirt road felt like the eyes of the devil himself taunting him. Pushing the pedal to the floor, he caught up to those enflamed eyes and prepared to smack them into oblivion. Instead, the eyes veered to the right, bounced back and forth and then disappeared. The haunting stare was there one second, gone the next, Holly and Abby along with it.

The humane part of him wanted to stop, needed to stop. The fear in him pushed him forward, down the road, and as far from the scene as possible. There were no witnesses. That is, until Abby Warren was pulled up the hill with her heart still beating. The only thing that had kept him out of prison that night was her silence. To make sure she kept it, he'd done everything in his power to force her out of town. With her departure, any evidence left behind on that dark country road ceased to matter, especially after the DNA samples were found to be contaminated. He'd walked away unscathed—guilty, responsible, mortified, but invisible and untouchable. A decade later, his false sense of security came to a grinding halt with Abby's return. He was positive she'd come home to break her silence.

A burning heat seared through his chest and he gripped the steering wheel tightly. Damn, this was not the time for his acid reflux to act up. Putting a hand to his chest, he lifted the lid of the console between the seats, digging through the mess inside to find a bottle of prescription acid reducer. Wrapping his fingers around it, he pulled it free of the compartment, popped the lid with his thumb and leaning his head back against the headrest, dropped two tablets directly from the bottle into his mouth. It took a couple of hard swallows, but he was finally able to get them down his throat.

By the time he closed the lid and threw the bottle back into the console, Gary Nelson was heading around the side toward the back of the building, his flashlight in hand while Joyce Warren pulled out of the parking lot and onto the main street. Without turning on his headlights, he put the truck into gear and began following the silver Sebring in front of him. He wasn't sure what his plan was, he only wanted to scare them. With that in mind, he flipped on the bright lights and pressed his foot down on the accelerator until he was mere inches from their back bumper. The car immediately swerved from left to right before increasing speed. It was a clear indication they knew he was there.

He clinched his jaw together making his teeth grind bone against bone. His adrenaline began to pump faster as he closed the distance Joyce had created between them. They were bumper to bumper now, the little car swerving back and forth on the paved two-lane street. Those familiar red eyes glared at him while he tried his best to anticipate her moves and followed closely behind. Suddenly, the car picked up pace once again, putting more distance between them. Before he could catch up, the brake lights flashed with taunting smugness and she turned the corner. The turn was too fast and he watched the car lean heavily to the right. He was certain only two wheels were connected with the ground. Joyce tried to recover the out of control turn but couldn't and ended up forcing the nose of her car into the drainage ditch on their left. The vehicle came to an abrupt stop as a thick gray smoke snaked its way over the top of the hood.

Gasping a deep breath, he floored the accelerator and drove straight past the intersection as he raced away from them. His heart was pounding in his chest. Internally, he fought the basic need to flee, but he was still human and couldn't help feeling an anxious desire to go back and confirm both women were okay. The conflicting emotions troubled him. It was the same thing he'd felt all those years ago when Holly's car had raced down that ravine. He was on a slow downward spiral and losing control. Suddenly, he didn't know how to keep his past from blowing up his future.

It was dark when Chad finally climbed into the cab of his truck. He loved his mother and would do anything for her, but he'd wanted to hit the road over an hour ago. The thought of seeing Abby, of holding her against him, had him in a state of agitation he hadn't felt in years. He swore he could smell the fresh scent of her shampoo like she'd been sitting in the seat next to him only seconds ago. He thought his infatuation with her in high school had been bad, but this was ten times worse. With a shake of his head, he turned the key and the truck rumbled to life.

He was only fifteen blocks, a host of small squares that housed a maximum of four properties each, away from her. Still, it felt as though they were miles apart in distance. Backing the truck out of the driveway, he shifted into gear and pushed the accelerator to the floor. The transmission jolted slightly from the swift change and the tires barked on the asphalt pavement as the vehicle thrust forward. The breeze from the open window blew warm air over his face, ruffling his dark hair. Letting loose of the steering wheel with one hand, he pushed the annoying strands out of his eyes.

He barreled down a narrow, two-lane street while a vision of Abby's face flashed in front of him instead of the terrain ahead. A streetlight overhead flickered, catching his attention, and went black as he drew near. Only eight more blocks to go. The tension in his shoulders began to ease. He'd hated leaving her alone for the day. Well, not necessarily alone, she'd been with her mother, but Joyce couldn't protect her nearly as well as he could. Suddenly those fierce defenses flared and the easing tension rebounded, tightening once again. He gripped his fingers around the wheel, flexing the muscles that wound up the length of his arm. Abby deserved so much more than this town had ever given her. He shook his head, drew in a deep breath, and came to an abrupt stop in front of the Warren house.

Climbing down from the truck, he noted that Joyce's car was missing from the gravel drive. He briefly wondered if she'd gone back to the hospital and left Abby alone as he stalked across the yard using wide strides in order the reach the back porch quickly. His heart beat with excitement as he closed the distance between them. The porch light was on, helping him to maneuver past the landscaping surrounding the wraparound porch, as was the kitchen light. He didn't notice the note taped to the door until he was in front of it. Snatching it, tape and all off the window pane, he held it in front of him.

Chad,

The police received an anonymous call that someone broke into the lumberyard. Mom and I have gone to meet Deputy Nelson there. Sit tight, we'll be back shortly.

Abby

Sit tight? Not a chance. Chad crumpled the paper in his hand and bounded off the porch, clearing the bottom step by a good three feet. As soon as his boots hit the ground he was running toward the truck, his heart pounding frantically within his chest. Blood and adrenaline pumped furiously through his body as he threw open the door and leapt into the cab. Somehow he slammed it shut, started the engine, and shoved the gearshift into drive all at the same time. Stomping down on the accelerator once again, the truck rolled forward without the slightest hiccup. Feeling like Batman in the Batmobile, he raced down the street, rounded the corner, and headed north toward the lumberyard at a speed the police would happily write him a ticket for.

Chapter Thirteen

A SOUND REVERBERATED through the vehicle's interior as Abby locked her arms in front of her, keeping distance between her body and the dashboard as the hood of the car slammed into the grass and weed packed earth. Her throat felt raw and she realized the sound resonating around her must have been her own scream. A scream born of terror, she was certain, as this could not be happening all over again. A cold, prickly sweat broke across her body as she recalled a similar night when she'd been forced off the edge of Three Mile Road. With huge eyes that looked black in the dark interior of the car, she gazed at her mother's slack form as she lay with her torso slumped over the steering wheel. Her heart skipped a beat. "Mom!" Abby shouted as she reached over and began shaking her mother's shoulder. "Mom, are you okay?"

Memories of Holly sprawled against the door all those years ago assaulted her. It hadn't been the drop into the ravine that had killed her; it was the broken tree limb that had smashed through the window and into her skull. The shattered glass had exploded, landing everywhere. Abby remembered the tiny cuts it left behind on her arms and legs and she'd had to pick it out of her hair for days. Those long, dark moments had been horrific. She recalled the blank stare on Holly's face and the way her eyes had gazed off into the distance, devoid of life. She hadn't suffered. One moment she had been there, the next, she was gone. Abby had always been thankful for her peaceful exit. Her own life had taken a turn in the opposite direction. She hadn't met with a truly peaceful moment until she'd found herself wrapped in Chad Austin's arms four days ago. The sadness of it was as disheartening as it was thrilling.

Her gaze focused again upon her mother's flaccid form. She would not allow her to follow Holly's fate. With her heart beating a frantic rhythm that threatened to barrel directly through her thoracic cage, she gasped for breath. Blackness began creeping its way around the edges of her vision, working at stealing away her consciousness. She fought against giving into it. She had to stay awake. She had to make sure her mother was okay. Giving her head a good shake helped to clear the fog and engage her vision.

Abby worked her fingers over the thick black polyester seatbelt, sliding them back to the locking mechanism. The push button of the lock was stuck, refusing to release her. She tugged at the seatbelt crossed over her right shoulder and worked diagonally across her chest. It wouldn't budge. "Mom," she cried, fighting tears of frustration that were springing into the corners of her eyes. Fear raced through her as she tore at the clasp, forcing the release button down again and again.

Finally, the latch gave way and she fell forward, her chest hitting the dashboard with a force that nearly knocked the wind out of her. She groaned as she moved her legs which were now awkwardly pinned beneath her. Using her upper body strength, she managed to push herself backward and turn toward the driver's seat. With trembling limbs, she reached out to run her fingers over her mother's throat, checking for a pulse. The warmth of her mother's skin washed over her tentative touch and she was assured the beat beneath her fingertips was strong and steady. Huge tears born of agonized angst flooded uncontrollably down her cheeks.

She curled her body into a fetal position next to her mother and gave into them.

Abby sat there with her eyes tightly closed long after the torrent of emotional overload had subsided. The car was abnormally quiet, the only sound being their combined breathing. Though she knew the outcome was different, it was the same silence she'd felt buried at the bottom of that deadly ravine with Holly and it was disturbing. Her chin began to tremble with the onslaught of her memories. The lost hopelessness, the infinite betrayal, the blatant lies had all swirled around her, swallowing up her youthful innocence. Those lies had barricaded themselves deeply within her and she wasn't certain that even the truth could set her free.

"Joyce!" The hoarse words were accompanied by a heavy pounding of a fist on the glass of the back window.

Startled, Abby flinched.

Joyce groaned.

"Mom," she said, stroking her mother's forehead, tracing her fingers over a huge knot that had surfaced there.

"Abby?" the deep voice sounded again from outside of the car.

"Yes," she answered, relieved to find that help had arrived.

"Are you okay?"

"A little shaken up," she said. "Mom hit her head."

"Can you unlock the door for me?"

Abby managed to move, reaching her body across the interior to press the button on the passenger's side door. The locks popped up allowing the gathering crowd access to them. When the passenger door swung open Donnie Burke hunkered down in the ditch to get a look inside. Abby fought off more tears as she looked into his familiar face, noting the concerned gaze.

"Hey Squirt," he said, giving her a quick smile as he tried to put her at ease.

"Mom?" Abby glanced back over her shoulder, completely ignoring the childhood endearment.

"It's okay. Gary's got her," Donnie said, reaching a hand toward her. "Let me help you out of there."

Abby stumbled gracelessly across the expanse of space between them. When she got close enough, Donnie snaked a solid, musclebound arm around her waist and lifted her toward him. In fact, her feet never reached the ground until they were standing on the asphalt. While he steadied her with a firm hand to each side of her waist, she blinked her eyes as she took in the spectacle before her. The front end of the car was wedged into a three-foot drainage ditch. The back tires were not even touching the ground. They were lucky they hadn't been hurt any worse than they had.

"Abby, are you okay?" Donnie asked, gazing cautiously at her.

"I think so," she said, slowly testing her arms and legs. "My shoulder is sore but I'm sure it's from the seatbelt."

"You'll probably have quite a nice bruise tomorrow."

"If that's the worst of it, then I'm good."

Donnie smiled an uneasy smile at her and then turned his gaze to watch Gary Nelson move out of the way, allowing the volunteer EMT's to do their jobs. A man dressed in jeans, a white T-shirt, and dark blue jacket with a business emblem embroidered on the left chest pocket knelt down beside her mother. Abby could hear him speaking to her but couldn't decipher the words. It was several long, tense moments before he and Gary Nelson slowly pulled her to her feet. Normally, Abby thought, they would have put a brace around her neck and belted her to a backboard, or maybe she had simply watched too many cop shows on her seven-channel television and had made that assumption incorrectly.

"Abby?" Joyce asked as they crested the ditch and stepped onto the street beside them. She wobbled slightly but there was no way to misinterpret the worry that was clearly etched across her features.

"I'm all right," Abby said, moving toward her with outstretched arms. The two women embraced forcefully leaving the rescue party to do nothing but stand back and view the humbling reunion.

———=«(●)»=———

Chad rolled the passenger window down to force some air through the cab as the single window wasn't doing much good at cooling the thick sheen of perspiration that clung to him. The knowledge that something was very wrong had his gut clinched into a tight ball. He could barely breathe as he punched the accelerator pedal, causing the truck to lurch forward unnaturally. The lumberyard was only a couple of blocks east of town square. At the intersection of Sycamore and Third, he made a hasty right onto Redwood and then a quick left onto Fourth which would take him into town.

He could see the red flickering lights in the distance before he reached the commotion. A police car, an ambulance, and a tow truck were lining Nash Street, blocking any evidence of why they were there from his view. He abruptly applied the brake and turned left to join them. Pulling to a stop on the side of the street, he jammed the gear into park, pulled the keys from the ignition, and jumped out sprinting toward the gathered crowd. The first person he encountered was Karl Dunkin. "Hey, Karl, what's going on?" he asked, fighting to keep the fear racing through his body out of his voice.

"Hey Chad," Karl replied. "I was called in to pull Joyce Warren's car out of the ditch."

"I think Abby was with her, are they okay?"

"Joyce is in the ambulance, she's got a nice goose-egg on her forehead. I saw Abby with Donnie Burke that way," he said, pointing his finger straight ahead.

"Thanks," Chad said with a nod as he took off at a quick gait.

He passed Gary Nelson who was talking with a bystander, a homeowner presumably, but he didn't stop to verify which one. Next he viewed the ambulance with Joyce Warren sitting on a gurney inside, answering questions for the EMT. In front of the ambulance, he found Donnie Burke with his arm wrapped around Abby's shoulders in supportive fashion as she sat on the downturned tailgate of his truck. With a brown blanket around her, she looked like a frightened child and he couldn't seem to get to her fast enough. "Abby!" he shouted.

Both Abby and Donnie turned to acknowledge him at the same moment. Her eyes were huge, her features tight. The look terrified him and he couldn't take his gaze off of her.

"Hey, Chad," Donnie said quietly as he approached.

Chad didn't respond, he simply walked up to Abby and pulled her shaking frame solidly into his embrace. "I'm here," he said softly, angling her body toward him. "I'm right here."

She sagged against him as though all life had drained from her body. Then, she began to sob. He looked over her shoulder to meet Donnie's worried gaze and snuggled her closer. He knew that she was reliving those tormenting moments from long ago. Though it wasn't the same outcome as that fateful day ominously living in her memories, it didn't help lessen the fear that pumped through her veins. He needed to know what had happened to put them in the ditch. The questions burned in his throat one after another but he kept silent, stroking her back with one hand while holding her tight with the other.

Suddenly, she worked her hands in front of her and pushed him back. Not hard, but enough to put a few inches of space between them. She settled onto the tailgate and swiped at the remaining tears still trickling down her cheeks. She looked at him then, swiftly moving her gaze to Donnie and back to him. She sniffled loudly, trying to clear her throat.

Chad laid the palms of his hands on her knees. "What happened?" he asked.

"Someone ran us off the road," she said. Her voice was strong and laced with a twinge of anger.

"Do you know who it was?"

"Someone in a dark pickup truck."

"But you don't know who?"

"No," she said with a shake of her head. "I'm sure they followed us from the lumberyard."

"Did they hit you?"

She gave another adamant shake of her head. "No, they turned their bright lights on and tailgated us. Mom tried to get away by turning the corner but she lost control of the car and we ended up in the ditch. Whoever it was just drove off and left us there."

Chad groaned out loud. How could anyone do something so horrendous? It was an extremely disturbing act for him to understand. He couldn't even begin to decipher how Abby was coping with it. It simply made no sense. Why would someone needlessly bring unwanted attention to himself? They had gotten away with murder ten years ago, so why continue the harassment when Abby had said nothing incriminating since her return? He, whoever he was, was the one responsible for the police involvement, not Abby.

Deputy Nelson stepped in between Donnie and Chad, his dark brown uniform slightly dusty. "We're done with the preliminary investigation. If it's okay with you, Abby, we're going to let Karl pull the car out of the ditch and tow it to the body shop," he said.

She gave a stiff nod of her head. "That's fine."

"Your mother is refusing a ride to the hospital. You'll need to keep an eye on her tonight, she may have a concussion."

"I'll keep an eye on both of them," Chad said.

"You don't—"

"Don't even go there," he said, stopping Abby midsentence. "I will be staying tonight."

Chad couldn't help but observe the amused looked that bounced between Gary Nelson and Donnie Burke as Abby lowered her head and shrugged her shoulders in defeat. The corners of Chad's mouth tilted upward ever so slightly. The matter was settled.

———————

An hour later, Abby was pacing in the living room waiting for Chad to return from a quick run home, the events of the past few days vividly swimming in her mind. It couldn't be a coincidence, could it? First her car and now this, it was too much. The more she thought about it, dissected it, the more assured she was that tonight had been a set up. There was no one snooping around the lumberyard. The call had only been a ruse to get her out of the house, to put her in a vulnerable position and scare her into leaving all over again. However, it wasn't going to happen this time. She was not the same naïve, immature, barely graduated from high school girl who'd run away from Mills Pond. She'd grown up and taken control of her life, refusing now to relinquish everything she'd become because her return made someone nervous.

Of that, she was positive. Someone was worried about her intention. Abigail Warren had arrived home, whole, not broken. Someone had secrets and meant to keep them buried, no matter what the cost to her or her family. Her adrenaline, finally calmed from the last bout of excitement, began to skyrocket once again. There was someone in Mills Pond who had been out on Three Mile Road that night, someone responsible for Holly's death. Someone else knew the truth and he was coming after her. Abby's breath began coming in swift, shallow gasps. She sat down on the blue and yellow plaid couch and put her head between her knees in an effort to keep at bay the blackness swooping down around her.

"Abby," her mother said, sitting down beside her. "Are you okay?"

She felt her mother's cool fingers trailing across her back, up her spinal cord and wrapping around her hair, pulling it back from her face. Tears sprang unwittingly to her eyes. This gentle, parental comforting was something she had missed for too many years gone by. They had commiserated on the phone, but there was just something about a mother's touch that both soothed and calmed. There was so much love conveyed in that moment, Abby let her guard down and succumbed to it.

Chapter Fourteen

CHAD HADN'T WANTED to leave Abby and Joyce, even for a moment. Donnie Burke had agreed to stand guard at the Warren house while he ran home to throw a change of clothes and a few toiletries into an overnight bag. He'd managed to make the round trip in less than thirty minutes. He was now standing in the Warren's bright yellow kitchen watching Abby remove a steaming mug of water from the microwave with shaking hands. With three quick strides of his long legs, he was at her side, offering assistance. "Here, let me take that," he said, moving his fingers over the tops of hers. Her chin trembled as she released her hold.

"I wanted a cup of tea," she said, her voice soft, distracted.

He nodded his head. "Where are the tea bags?" he asked, quickly placing the cup on the counter before he burned his fingers. His gaze shifted in her direction, watching her move to open a cabinet to their left. She pulled out a box of apple spiced tea bags and a glass jar of honey. Setting both of them onto the counter in front of her, she stared at them absently.

"Abby?"

She slowly looked up at him, blinking her eyes. He assumed she was trying to keep her tears at bay. He couldn't imagine what was going through her head. "I'm sorry," she said.

He abandoned the hot cup of water and moved to wrap his arms around her. She stepped into his embrace willingly, her body fitting against his like a missing puzzle piece. It made his chest seize in some crazy unfamiliar way. Her rapid breathing didn't help calm the situation.

"Chad," she said with her face flush against his chest.

"Hmmm?" he asked in a questioning fashion as actual words were having a hard time surfacing.

"I think it was Chase's truck."

The air in his lungs froze. The idea was something that had been floating around in the back of his mind. To hear the words out loud brought them alive and crackled in the space surrounding them. As much as he wanted to deny the possibility, he couldn't. Their discussion earlier today had left him at odds with Chase and any doubts of his brother's innocence, especially now, were tangible. Still, Chase was his brother and he didn't want to believe that he may be capable of something like this. "But you don't know for sure?"

She pulled back slightly to look up into his face. Her pale skin and wary features were a clear indication of the trauma she'd experienced. "Can I prove it was him? No," she said, her eyes flashing with resolute intensity. "Not with any certainty. But who else could it be?"

"Baby," he said, his arms sliding up her back as he hooked his hands over her shoulders, "I don't know. But I promise you, we will find out who it is."

Her lips trembled before the words tumbled across them. "And if it is Chase, what are you going to do?"

He met her gaze directly. "Whoever is responsible will be brought to justice."

"Even if it is Chase?" she asked.

He gave a solid nod of his head. "Yes, even if it's Chase."

She closed her eyes and he pulled her fully against him once more.

Abby had fallen into bed late and spent the remainder of the night in fitful bursts of sleep while Chad had kept watch over them from the comfort of the couch one floor below. By the light of morning, she'd agreed to accompany her mother to the hospital. It was awkward as she hadn't spoken to her father since her abrupt departure from home a decade ago. *Home*—that was a funny word to use but what else was there? Her parent's house was the only home she'd ever known. An apartment was just an apartment, cold and lonely. A home was warm and inviting. It was a place where love bonded, laughter abounded, and family thrived. She'd been thoroughly loved once in this place and she vowed to be again. She was determined to find a way to repair the damage that had been inflicted, no matter what it took.

She hadn't cried over her circumstance in years but coming back had changed that. It was as though Roto-Rooter had made a surprise visit and now her dehydrated tear ducts had sprung an incessant leak. Life's lessons should have toughened her up more. She certainly hadn't been prepared for the vast overload of grief that visiting Holly's gravesite had caused, let alone the dam of pent-up emotions she'd allowed to crack and gush all over Chad Austin and his pristine wooden floors. It was an emotional drain she'd struggled to control. But last night had changed things. In her meeting with the ditch, she'd found her missing inner-strength and there was no putting the stopper back in the bottle. It was simply too late. Twice was one time too many. She was ready to face life head on in whatever capacity she needed to in order to find happiness. She had earned the right to be happy.

Forcing herself to take a deep breath, she marched into the dismal white hospital room like a woman on fire. Her mother had agreed to give her a few moments alone with her father and she planned to take full advantage of it. Paul Warren's head turned when she stepped through the doorway, the burnt sienna color of his eyes glittering in a way she couldn't quite decipher.

"Abigail," he said softly.

A hard knot formed in Abby's throat as she stood affixed to a spot only a couple of feet inside the doorway. She felt like a very small child seeking love and approval from the man who, from the moment she was born, had been her hero. This was the man who had shaped and sharpened her view of the world. This was the man she'd worshipped as a child. His was the lap she had crawled onto when she was frightened. His were the hands that had gently played with her and firmly disciplined her when necessary. She'd sought his smile and attention at every turn. And when her young adult world had blown up, she'd learned the full wrath of his disappointment. If she was honest with herself, she'd have to admit that his irritation and denial of her innocence had played as big a part in her decision to leave Mills Pond as Chase Austin had. She simply couldn't stand the sad look in his eyes. That she'd even remotely let him down had left a huge empty hole in her heart for far too many years.

With the knowledge that she'd never been able to relinquish that feeling, she swallowed and forced herself to move forward. "Hello, Dad," she said, the timber of her voice quivering slightly in her nervousness.

Tears welled in his eyes, making them glassy as he gazed at her. She watched a train of droplets glide down his sallow cheeks as they escaped the wrinkled skin surrounding the wide-set of his oval-shaped lids. She dragged in another ragged breath in an effort to slow her erratically beating heart, feeling it burn her throat as she forced the air down. Fighting off tears of her own, she curled her fingers into fists, digging her blunt nails into the skin of her palms. It didn't help. The tears came anyway. When he lifted his arms welcoming refuge from a drought created from a decade of lost time, she moved quickly, bending her knees and settling into a seated position on the small mattress of the steel gray hospital bed beside him. Abby buried her face into the crook where his neck and shoulder met as he slid his arms around her. "Oh, Daddy," she cried. "I'm so sorry."

"Shhh," he whispered, holding onto her trembling form a little more tightly. "You're home. That's all the matters."

His words only made her tears fall faster. With the sobering comfort of his arms around her, she began to sob harder. Her relationship with her mother had always come effortlessly. Not to say they hadn't had their fair share of disagreements—they had—but Joyce had attended her college graduation and also visited her in St. Louis. There were more disappointments during the annual holiday season but they'd managed to maintain their relationship, albeit at a distance. Her father, on the other hand, had refused to leave the lumberyard. Abby knew it wasn't the business holding him at arm's length. It was his animosity toward her decision to leave that had kept him away. Now that she'd finally come home, she intended to fully rectify the situation. No halfway for her. She wasn't budging until they were on solid footing once more.

Abby gulped in another deep breath of air in an effort to squelch the crying jag. Her body fought the attempt and a string of hiccups set in, causing her to quake with subtle jerks. At last, she lifted her head to gaze at him, meeting the reflection of her soaked, swollen face within the dark depths of his gaze. "Hi, Dad," she whispered.

"Ah, Abby," he said, a comforting smile breaking across his face, softening the hardened features of their last encounter. "It's good to see you."

She took in his ashen face, slimmer than she remembered. His dark hair now held more gray than brown. He was a large man, tall and broad. She had gotten her height from him, along with his straight aristocratic nose, thick hair, fair skin, and double-jointed fingers. He had aged slightly but was still the man she'd always loved. While sitting beside him, it wasn't hard to imagine her as a rambunctious four year old, climbing the ladder to the roof of the house where he was repairing a few loose shingles. Her trusty plastic farm animal embellished lunchbox in hand. She had been determined to share her peanut butter and jelly sandwich with the only man in the world who mattered. She smiled at the memory. "It's good to see you too."

He used the gnarled knuckle of his index finger to gently caress beneath her chin. "If I'd known this is all it would have taken to get you to come home, I would've injured myself a long time ago."

Abby audibly groaned at his statement. How could he so easily make light of their decade of cool detachment?

"Help me up," he said, struggling to pull himself to a sitting position. "I need to sit in the chair."

Abby stood up and glanced from him to the green vinyl recliner beside her. "Are you sure you want me to help you do this?" she asked.

"Yes," he said, pushing the stiffly starched white blanket to the side. His right knee was swollen to the size of a large cantaloupe and he had stitches on both his upper and lower leg where the skin had been torn away. The knee itself was thickly bandaged and resting on a stack of pillows. His foot was so swollen it looked like it might explode. "You'll have to help me slide around so I'm facing you," he instructed. "Pull my left leg toward you and turn at the same time."

Abby reached beneath the navy blue shorts covering his left leg and slowly began to pivot his body toward the bed's edge in front of her. When he winced, she loosened her hold but he caught her left hand, prodding her to continue. Soon, he was sitting on the bed sideways; his good leg bent properly, the sole of his bare foot resting on the cold gray tile floor. The injured leg stuck straight out in front of him. He leaned back with his arms behind him, his chest heaving heavily beneath the white cotton of the T-shirt he wore.

"Do you need to rest?" she asked.

"No, I'm okay. Help me over to the chair."

Abby carefully sat down to his right, next to his injured leg. Placing her shoulder under his arm, she used the full extent of her weight to guide him to a standing position. He wrapped his arm tightly around her trunk, using her body as a crutch; they maneuvered the few steps of space between the bed and the chair. She then helped him to turn around and eased him down onto the padded cushion of the seat.

"Thank you," he said, leaning against the back of the chair. His voice was the slightest bit harsh as he dealt with the offending pain of being jostled. She wasn't very good at nursing. "Can you help me put the leg-rest up?"

Abby reached down and slowly pulled the lever on the side of the chair forward. It eased back as the leg-rest lifted into position. "What else can I do?" she asked.

"Well look at the two of you." At the sound of her voice, Abby turned to find her mother standing in the doorway, a soft smile curving her lips.

Abby wondered briefly how long their reunion had been spied upon. "Hi."

"Looks like everything is under control here," Joyce said, stepping into the room. Without hesitation, her mother walked over to her father and planted a kiss on the top of his head. "How are you feeling?"

"Tired," he responded.

"Well, you've got a little more time to relax. The physical therapist is running late. She'll be here this afternoon."

"Fine," he said, a bit gruffly. "I could use a break."

"No pun intended?" her mother asked.

Paul chuckled in answer to her question.

Joyce shook her head and turned to look in Abby's direction. "I'm going to stay for a while if you want to head on over to the office."

Abby nodded her head. "Okay," she said, knowing full well that her mother wanted to share with him the news of last night's accident. That was fine with her. She didn't want to think about it anymore.

"I'll stop by after the physical therapist gets here."

Abby looked from her mother to her father. "I'll catch up with you both later."

Her mother smiled again and mouthed the words *thank you* as she walked past them on the way to the door.

"Abby?"

She stopped and turned toward her father. "Yes?"

"It really is good to have you home," he said, smiling briefly as he slid his hand against her mother's as she sat down on the bed across from him.

"Thank you." They were the only words she could muster before hurrying from the room. The elevator ride to the lobby was a blur and her heart was still pounding when she walked out of the building in a rush for her car. She'd convinced herself that seeing her father would be another tough experience and was stunned when she'd encountered his gentle manner and simple kindness instead. It angered her just a bit as she pulled away from her parking space. She'd been certain that he'd disowned her all those years ago and had prepared herself to meet his wrath. Instead, he'd offered compassion. His response threw her equilibrium off. She was irritated and relieved at the same time. It was an oddly mixed sensation. Thankfully, she had a fifteen minute drive before arriving at the lumberyard. She hoped it was long enough to diminish the overwhelming surge of emotion currently bombarding her.

Chapter Fifteen

LETTING ABBY GO that morning had been one of the most difficult decisions Chad had made in some time. Keeping watch over both of the Warren women had given him immense satisfaction. Somehow, and he wasn't quite sure how, he'd even managed to bond with that darned hunk of orange tabby she'd hauled into town with her. He'd woken up in the middle of the night with Brewtus sprawled out comfortably across his chest, snoring. A slight smile tugged at the corners of his mouth at the memory. He didn't think that a normal cat snored. However, there was nothing normal about his relationship with Abby Warren.

The sultry breeze trailing inside the open window of the truck blew across his face. Though the sun still hung low in the morning sky, the thick heated air was a sure sign that the day ahead would be sweltering. He pulled into the parking lot of the Mills Pond High School and aimed in the direction of the football field. Moving across the loose gravel lot, he spotted Chase's black Ford F150 pickup in the teacher's parking lot located closer to the building. Knowing his brother as well as he did, Chad assumed Chase was already on the field making last minute changes to his practice roster. They had about twenty minutes before the team swarmed out of the locker room and onto the open field. He hoped it would be enough time for another tense discussion.

Spotting Chase on the far side of the field, Chad climbed out of the cab and shut the door behind him. Though the stadium was empty, he couldn't help but evoke a rush of excitement as he walked. It was almost possible to feel the twinge of electricity brought on by a game, one he hadn't been part of for a long time. It didn't matter. Memories of the crisp fall air, the bright lights overhead, and the eager enthusiasm of a packed house made a shiver of pride race down his spine. Magic happened in this stadium. At least it had for him.

The closer he drew, the clearer Chase's features became. He was absorbed in the paperwork attached to his clipboard, completely oblivious to his surroundings. Typically there would be nothing going on before practice but today was not an ordinary day. The accusations toward his brother were swiftly mounting and he had come for answers. Chad noted Chase's relaxed stance as he took in the khaki shorts and light blue Polo shirt he wore. He had on a maroon ball cap which snapped upward when Chad drew close.

"What are you doing here?" Chase asked in an annoyed tone.

"We need to talk," Chad said.

"I thought we did that yesterday."

Chad pulled to a stop in front of his brother and crossed his arms over his chest. "We did."

"Look," Chase said, dropping the clipboard to his side," I've got nothing else to say."

"Too bad, I've got more questions."

Chase expelled a sharp breath of heated air from his lungs. "I've got a practice to run."

"Where were you last night?" Chad asked, ignoring the dismissive air in his brother's voice.

Chase looked down and scribbled something on the clipboard. "What's it to you?"

"There was an accident last night," he said, barely holding his anger in check.

"Let me guess," Chase said flippantly.

Chad took a full step in Chase's direction, his chest solidly bumping the clipboard.

"Hey," Chase complained. "I'm working here."

Gripping the clipboard in one hand, Chad yanked it out of Chase's hands and dropped it onto the ground. "Let me start over," he said, meeting his brother's wary gaze straight on. "Someone forced Joyce Warren off the road and into a ditch last night after a false claim was made about a break-in at the lumberyard. Abby was with her and it's rumored that a dark truck that looks a lot like yours was responsible."

Chase stared back at him, his eyes piercing while his lids held fast without so much as a blink. "It wasn't me," he said forcefully.

"Where were you?"

"None of your business," Chase said.

"I drove by your house last night and your truck wasn't there," Chad said in an accusatory manner.

Chase's jaw drew taut. "It wasn't me," he repeated. "Besides, this town has its fill of mysterious dark trucks."

"This has gone far enough, Chase," Chad growled. "I don't care what kind of jilted anger you still carry for Abby; the stalking has to stop before someone really gets hurt."

Chase snorted, the loud echo of sound hung in the air. "Are you not listening?" he demanded.

"Oh, I'm listening and reading between the lines."

"Whatever," Chase said, shaking his head.

Chad could hear the commotion as a group of young men trotted across the field, ready to commence their morning practice. He reached his left hand out to grip Chase's bicep. "I won't let you continue this."

Chase shrugged him off. "You have no proof it was me."

"Not yet," Chad said. "But I will. And when I do, so help me—"

"You'll what?" Chase said, meeting his gaze and holding it for a long moment. Finally in a dismissive tone, he said, "I've got a practice to run."

"This isn't over," Chad said, his aggravation clear.

Chase turned toward the team of football players awaiting direction from him. After a couple of steps, he turned back and bent to snatch the clipboard off the ground. "If you really want to know, I was playing poker last night."

Chad shook his head. "Right."

"There were eight of us. You can ask any of them," Chase continued, then pulled a roll of Tums out of his pocket and popped a couple of tablets into his mouth before turning on his right heel and jogging toward his team.

Chad felt an outlandish fear pounding away inside his chest like an angry sea slamming against a mountain of rock. He couldn't breathe as he turned his back to the field and walked away. He certainly didn't want Chase to be guilty of bringing harm to the woman he'd fallen head over heels for, but in all honesty, Chase had given him nothing concrete to prove that he wasn't involved. In fact, he'd given quite the opposite impression. If anything were to happen to Abby, God help the person responsible.

— ◈ —

It had been an odd day. Abby had spent it mulling over the early morning reunion with her father and still felt off kilter. And now, she sat Indian style on a blanket at the edge of the creek, directly across from Chad. He'd put a nice picnic dinner together for them. Chicken salad from the diner, a mixed assortment of cheese and crackers and a cluster of huge green grapes, all of which they'd barely touched. Instead, she lifted the cold bottle of Bud Light to her lips, feeling the cooling rush of liquid gently glide down her throat while she gazed at him sprawled lengthwise across one side of the blanket. One of his arms was propped beneath his head, the other rested on the top of her knee.

"You haven't said much about the visit with your dad," he said as he traced a circle around her kneecap with his thumb.

She blew out a slow breath. "No, I haven't."

"Did it go okay?"

Abby leaned to the left, placing the beer bottle in the grass at the edge of the blanket. She kept her eyes focused downward as she straightened and pulled both hands into her lap, clasping her fingers together. "It was strange," she finally said.

"What do you mean?" he asked in a voice gone soft with question.

She looked up, her tongue darting out to wet her bottom lip as she gazed at him. "The reunion wasn't what I'd expected."

His palm shifted around her kneecap once again. "How so?"

She swallowed as her thoughts rushed together in her head. "He was so disappointed in me before I left. So much so that I couldn't handle the fact that I'd let him down. That coupled with the bullying was just too much. When I saw him today, after all these years of silence, he didn't show an ounce of animosity. He was just a man, a father who missed his daughter."

"That doesn't sound so bad," he said.

"I felt guilty and ashamed."

"What for?" he asked. "You haven't done anything."

"Exactly," she said with a heavy exhale. "He hasn't spoken to me in all this time so I didn't bother to speak to him either. What if I had? Would it have made a difference? Would we have tried to re-kindle our relationship sooner? Did I cause this too-long time warp because I got caught up in my pride?"

"No, Abby," Chad said. "I don't think he was disappointed in you, he was disappointed with himself."

Abby laughed a short chortle that caught in her throat. "Are we talking about the same man?"

Chad smiled at her, a quick upturn of his mouth that reached his eyes. "We are."

His smile was infectious and she couldn't help but return it.

"Abby, your dad loves you more than life itself. I've heard him talk about your college degree, your art work, and your life in St. Louis. He is very proud of you and your accomplishments. He's had to live with the mistake of letting you go for a long time."

Her stomach churned as her spirit soared. "You have?" she asked. "He really said those things about me?"

He laughed out loud. "Yes. It's time to put your guard down. Let him in, Abby. You need each other."

"So I'm being stupid?" she asked.

He laughed heartily and with a quick shake of his head, he reached out, hooking his arm behind her back and pulling her forward. She rolled and then tumbled toward him, her body somehow settling against the length of his as her hip rested upon the dirt packed earth beneath the blanket. His palm settled against her back as she looked up into his rugged features. The hint of the day's growth shadowed his jaw and chin. Spots of light glinted through the leaves of the tree limbs overhead catching a few strands of auburn in his hair. His body, warm and hard against hers, was as comforting as it was unnerving. His mouth dipped, pinning her lips against his and with a ragged sigh, she gave into the wondrous sensations he was creating.

Her breath caught in her throat as he rolled onto his back and pulled her with him, settling her on top of him. She could feel the heat and muscle beneath her and his arms wrapped around her, pulling her closer. Her body caught fire as his mouth ravaged hers over and over again. "Abby," he said in a whispered breath against her mouth.

"Yes?"

"I need you," he said.

Abby stilled her movements and opened her eyes. His pecan gaze was staring directly into hers. She slightly pulled her mouth back from his. "Here? Now?" she squeaked.

His face contorted, reflecting confusion. "What?" he asked.

"Are you telling me that you'd like to get naked on your lawn in broad daylight?"

"What?" he asked again.

"I need you?" she repeated.

His deep chuckle bewildered her even more.

"You don't—"

Chad placed his hand over her mouth, effectively terminating the flow of her words, his laughter still resounding in the air around them. "I'm sorry," he said. "I didn't mean I need you *now*, though the thought is very tempting."

She lightly punched his bicep with her right fist. "Then what did you mean?"

He reached up to catch her face between both palms. "Abby," he said with a sobered voice, "I need you in my life."

"Oh," she mouthed.

He smiled and slid her body to the blanket beside him. Sitting up, he guided her back to rest against his chest as he pointed toward the left side of the cabin. She followed the direction of his focus but saw only grass with a few scattered trees. Looking down at her, he continued. "Do you see that?"

"See what?" she asked, confused again by his question.

"The open space," he said, excitement lacing his voice.

"The grass?"

He gave her a huge smile. "Yes, the grass."

Abby nodded her head.

"I want to build you a state of the art workshop on that plot of land. You'd have a lot more room than a loft would provide and could create glass pieces to your heart's content."

Abby stared at him, not quite sure what to say. He really was working to include her in his life. Was she ready for a permanent relationship? Was it really possible to stay in Mills Pond and start completely over? Her breath came in quick gasps as she considered his offer.

"Abby, I want a family of my own and that begins with you and me."

She blinked back the moisture creeping into the corners of her eyes as a feeling of dark gloom descended. "How," she asked, "can you consider this when someone is trying to run me out of town?"

"We're going to put a stop to that."

"Whoever it is won't be happy that you're making long-term plans."

"Abby," he said, lowering his body back down beside hers. "Haven't you figured out yet just how crazy I am about you?"

She smiled. "Crazy is probably the right word."

He growled and pulled her to him once again, his mouth completely possessing hers. It felt so good that she let the worrisome edges of consciousness fade, allowing herself to be lost in the moment of magic he was creating. She only hoped that if his current plan was to get her naked, that they made it inside the house first.

Chapter Sixteen

DRIVING SLOWLY, HE pulled his truck onto a rutted dirt road, if you could call it that, about a quarter mile from Chad's house. It was tree-lined and went back a couple hundred feet or so, enough to hide the truck from any passersby. At this late hour he didn't expect any traffic, but in his mind, it was better to be safe than sorry. He shut off the lights, grabbed a flashlight along with a black canvas bag and climbed out of the cab, gently shutting the door behind him. Deciding against taking the road which was the easiest route, he headed across the choppy field in the direction of the house.

Under a tiny sliver of moonlight, he found the path to be a tricky one. The flashlight didn't illuminate the ground sufficiently and he tripped over clumps of overgrown weeds and dead carcasses of harvested root as he slowly worked his way over the field. From a distance, the house was dark. He'd checked the Warren driveway earlier and found it void of either car or truck, so Abby had gone to Chad tonight, not the other way around. As he gradually grew closer, he could make out the shape of Chad's truck in the drive-way. Surprisingly, there was no sign of Abby's little red Acura. He hadn't passed it on the way out of town so it must be parked in the garage. Either that or she wasn't here at all. It didn't matter and he truly didn't care. Tonight his focus was on Chad. The man's loyalty to the woman who was his enemy was getting out of hand and it was time to shut him down.

At the edge of the field, he turned the flashlight off, slung the bag over his shoulder, and quickly moved across the immaculate grassy yard toward the driveway. Once there, he maneuvered slowly, carefully climbing over the tailgate, inching his way toward the toolbox at the base of the truck bed. Pulling a coiled length of wire out of the back left pocket of his jeans, he jimmied the lock and pried it open. Sweat poured off his forehead while his heart pounded erratically. He'd thought himself above stealing but here he was, quietly lifting the lid to the treasure chest, helping himself to the tidy lot of loot inside. He began pulling out different sized mallets, a couple of chisels, a hand countersink, and a marking gauge. Digging deeper, he found a cloth kit of marking knives, a hardwood bevel, and a couple of framing squares. After loading all the gear into the black canvas bag and finding extra room, he found a couple of wrenches, a large set of pliers, and an electric drill. Stuffing those additions in, he could barely zip it closed.

Setting it to the side, he deliberately left the lid open and scooted his body back toward the tailgate while tugging the weighty bag of booty behind him. Climbing out of the truck was easy. Lifting out the heavy bag was not. Once he cleared the tailgate, he slung the strap across his chest and over his shoulder before trudging as quickly and quietly as possible back toward the field. The first step he took off the flat surface of the manicured lawn had him at a disadvantage as his right boot landed awkwardly in a deep hole and he twisted his ankle trying to dislodge it. Sucking in his breath to avoid a loud string of curses rushing into the darkness, he yanked it out and lumbered ahead hoping that this most recent attempt would be enough to sway Chad's interest away from Abby Warren.

———◦《◇》◦———

Abby was tallying inventory when her mother waltzed in bright and early the next morning. There was an air about her presence that caught Abby's attention as Joyce meted out greetings to customers and employees and made her way toward the office. Finishing up her count of flat corner irons, Abby closed the folder and moved in her mother's direction. Joyce was reviewing paperwork that had been left in a black wire rack on the corner of the desk when Abby walked in. "You're here early," she said.

Joyce looked up from a yellow delivery slip in her hand. "I've already been to the hospital and back this morning."

"How's Dad?"

Her mother smiled. "He's getting better every day. The doctor said he might be able to leave in a couple of days."

"What about his physical therapy?" Abby asked.

"He'll still get it. Someone from outpatient therapy will come to the house twice a day."

"That's good."

"I didn't hear you come in last night," her mother said, her interest in the subject apparent.

"I slept in my own bed," Abby confirmed, though she'd been tempted not to. His extremely potent kisses had nearly been her undoing and it had taken every ounce of her will power to walk away from the temptation that was Chad Austin.

Joyce raised one eyebrow.

"I am twenty-eight years old." Abby reminded her mother.

"Yes you are," Joyce said and then smiled. "I'm very happy for you, Abby."

"Chad told me last night that he wanted to build me an art studio on his property."

"Did he?" Joyce responded with animation.

Abby couldn't hold back the smile that erupted across her features as she nodded her head. The idea was crazy to contemplate but for the first time in a very long time, she wanted to do something irrational. Maybe that stemmed from the fact that she was finally surrounded by people who truly cared for her. The attachment to something beyond oneself was as remarkable as it was startling. She was tired of living a life of distance and solitude. She now had the chance to change some things—some very big things—and she sorely wanted to test the water.

"Does that mean you're thinking about staying?"

Abby nonchalantly shrugged her shoulders. "If we can uncover the mystery of who isn't a fan of my staying."

"Is that a yes?" her mother asked.

Abby smiled as her cheeks and throat turned a light shade of pink. "Yes," she said.

Joyce couldn't hide her enthusiasm as she burst into a smile. Even the spiky ends of her hair trembled with excitement.

A knock at the open door shifted their attention from their discussion as Chad poked his head inside. "Sorry to interrupt," he said.

With her smile still in place, Joyce trailed her gaze back and forth between them. "You're not interrupting. Come on in, Chad," she said with a wave of her hand.

With an anxious grace, he moved through the door and stood in front of them. "I apologize for dropping by so early."

Abby viewed the serious set of his features. Something was definitely off. "Is everything okay?" she asked.

With his full attention on her, he brought his body upright before answering. "Nothing happened after you left last night, did it?"

After an hour long discussion riddled with kisses meant to entice her into staying, she'd managed to convince him she could make it home safely. She had called him as soon as she'd arrived and they'd talked until late into the night. "No," she said with a quick shake of her head. "We had a quiet night."

He blew out a breath. "Good," he said.

The action convinced Abby that he was withholding information. "Did something happen?" she asked.

He gave a quick nod. "Someone broke into the toolbox in the back of my truck last night."

Joyce set the paperwork in her hand on the desktop. "Was anything taken?" she asked.

"Yes," he said, answering her mother's question but not moving his gaze from Abby. "Quite a lot, actually."

"Do you think it was because of me?" Abby asked.

"I don't know."

"No," Joyce said. "How could a theft like that be related to Abby? It couldn't. Could it?"

"My fear is that someone targeted me because they either feel they haven't scared you sufficiently or they're mad about my adamant pursuit of you."

"I'm sorry," Abby said, her voice faltering.

At once Chad closed the distance between them, pulling her against him. With a knuckle on his right hand, he lifted her chin so he could look her in the eye. "I didn't mean to blame you," he said. "If it is the same person, I'm happy they've moved their focus on to me."

Abby buried her face in his chest, partly because she wanted to and partly because he was forcing her there with the intensity of his embrace. Her heart was racing as he wrapped her tightly in his arms.

"Have you gone to the police?" Joyce suddenly demanded.

"No," Chad said with a shake of his head. "Not yet. I wanted to make sure there wasn't anything else to report."

"I think you should go right now, both of you."

Abby looked up into Chad's features once again. The skin over his cheekbones and jaw was drawn tight. "This has to stop," she said.

Chad nodded his head. "Yes, it does."

"Well go," Joyce said as she made shooing motions with her hands. "I'll stay here."

Catching Chad's hand in hers, Abby turned toward the door. "We'll be back as soon as we can."

"Good luck," her mother said. It was not difficult to discern the strain in her voice.

"We're going to need it," Abby replied as they walked past her and out the door.

━━━◈━━━

Even though the hardware store was only a few blocks from town square, Chad drove them to the city hall which housed the police station and courthouse in the same building. The two-story red brick office had been built in the late 1950's by Hudson Contracting. Hudson was responsible for constructing most of the commercial buildings in town square. Alford Hudson had been the sole owner until he'd closed up shop and retired at the age of eighty-one in 1992. He and his wife Edie had no children but planned to spend every ounce of their retirement doing all those things they'd passed up during the course of their business venture. Unfortunately, in the process of planning their well-earned, year-long cross-country motorhome trip, Alford died of a heart attack. Edie passed away less than a year later. A cement plaque of remembrance was affixed to the outer wall of the city hall as a permanent reminder of the well-loved couple.

Climbing the cement staircase beneath the black and white striped awning, Chad and Abby passed by the plaque. Reaching the door, Chad pulled the heavy glass frame open for her, giving a reassuring smile as she brushed past him. They were met with white paint and gray tile flooring as they stepped into the small reception area. There were two maroon office chairs sitting on either side of the door, giving the room a dot of color. Jamie Kilmer sat at the receptionist desk located between two open doorways. One led into the city hall and courthouse offices, the other into the police station. In her early twenties, Jamie was tall and thin with straight black hair and dark midnight blue eyes. Her face was long and angular which he thought weakened her attractiveness. Or maybe he was simply comparing her to Abby, in which case, the girl would never stand a chance.

Oblivious to his observation, she smiled up at him when he closed the door. "Hi Chad," she said. "Can I help you?"

"I'm looking for Chief Miller," he said.

Jamie nodded her head toward the left. "He should be in his office."

"Thanks," he said, hooking his fingers around Abby's waist and leading her in that direction.

Abby's body shuddered against the support of his arm. "Chief Miller never believed me."

His hand grasped at the indention of her waist, giving a subtle hint of encouragement. "It's going to be okay."

They moved through the doorway to find a large open workstation, partially walled-off in front leaving room for a four-foot long countertop and arched window space. Like the reception area, the white paint and gray tile flowed through the room. A line of black folding chairs sat forlornly against the left wall while black stenciling formed bold words above the arched window letting them know they had located the police station. Ellen Thayer stood up from her desk within the walled-off space and walked toward the counter that separated them. She was an older woman in her early sixties with a head full of gray hair that wildly curled about her round face. Her body was short and plump and the very reason she was perfectly cast as Mrs. Santa in the town's Christmas pageant every year. She'd worked for the police department for just over forty years. Neither snow, nor sleet, nor rain could keep her away from the job. Her husband Tom made darned sure of it. "Good morning, Ellen," he greeted.

"Why good morning, Chad," she said, absently touching her right hand to her gray curly mop. When she realized what she was doing, she dropped it and began tugging her pink top down over the flowered pink and white skirt.

He smiled a charming smile. "Do you remember Abigail Warren?" he asked.

Ellen smiled quickly in return. "Why yes, yes I do. It's a pleasure to see you again Abigail."

"Please call me Abby," she said.

"Of course," Ellen said. "What can I do for the two of you?"

"We're here to see Chief Miller." Chad informed her.

"I think he might be over at the café but let me check," Ellen said, heading through a door to their left and disappearing down the hallway.

It was crazy to think that the stolen tools in his truck were related to Abby in any way, but he couldn't shake the odd feeling hanging over him. He'd been angry when he'd discovered the broken tool box earlier that morning. Normally he parked his truck in the garage. He'd certainly tried to convince Abby to stay the night but was thankful now that she hadn't. There was no telling what might have happened to her car if it was left to sit in the driveway alongside his truck. He hoped he was just being paranoid after all that had happened and in reality, it was some random act of defiance delivered by a frustrated high school kid. He could deal with that notion much better than the alternative.

"Everything okay?"

Chad blinked his eyes to focus on the body the voice had come from. Gary Nelson stood in the doorway looking from him to Abby and back again. "Hey, Gary," Chad said.

"Is everything okay?" he asked again.

For some unknown reason, Abby took a step backward and her shoulders bumped against his chest. Chad caught his hands at either side of her waist to steady her but before he could decipher her reaction, Don Miller, the police chief stepped past Gary Nelson and into the room. He was dressed in the same brown trousers and shirt that his deputy wore, though with his larger size, his uniform fit more snuggly around his compact frame. The dark wavy hair was thinning on top and riddled with patches of gray. The deep lines set around his eyes and mouth gave his pewter gray gaze a piercing demeanor, especially when he looked in Abby's direction. It was no wonder she'd backed into him. His big voice boomed. "Chad, what can I do for you?"

At the sound, Abby jumped slightly. Chad was certain it wasn't evident to anyone but him, but he felt the dread roll off her in waves. Releasing one hand from her waist, he stepped up beside her and slid his right arm around her while keeping his gaze on the police chief. "Good morning, Chief Miller," he said. "I want to report a break-in and theft."

"A break-in?" both Chief Miller and Deputy Nelson said simultaneously.

"Someone broke the lockbox on my truck and helped themselves to the tools inside."

"When did this happen?" Gary asked.

"Last night," Chad answered.

"You'll need to file a report with Deputy Nelson," Chief Miller said. "I presume you know what's missing?"

Chad nodded his head. "Yes I do."

"Very good. Gary, take the report." Chief Miller ordered and turned his back on them.

"Chief," Chad said, stopping the man mid-stride. "We'd like to talk to you about something else as well."

"What is it?" he asked, turning back toward them.

"I'm sure you know that someone has been harassing Abby?"

Chief Miller scowled and crossed his arms over his thick chest. "What did you expect after all this time?" he asked, his gaze directed at Abby.

"Excuse me?" she said.

"You left town in a quite hurry ten years ago, Abigail. You have to agree that your quick departure looked suspect. Did you think the town was going to hold a parade in your honor the minute you came back?"

"No Sir," Abby said. "But as I recall, I was found to be innocent of any wrong doing."

Chief Miller glared at her with his critical gray eyes, his mouth following suit with an even darker glower. "As I recall, the only thing you were found to be not guilty of that evening was alcohol consumption. The car you were driving still left the roadway and killed an innocent woman in the process."

Chad heard Abby's swift intake of breath at the same moment the man's words slammed into his gut. "That's enough," he said. "We didn't come here to be accosted by the Chief of Police."

Chief Miller laughed out loud. "Accosted?" he said. "Sooner or later, the truth catches up. You'd best be wary of that," he said, his sharp gaze meeting Chad's stunned features.

"You wouldn't know the truth if it—"

"Abby!" Chad quickly jumped in to shut the offhanded comment down. "Let's go file that report with Deputy Nelson, okay?"

He heard her choke off the end of her sentence but completely understood her irritation of the treatment she'd received. It was no wonder she'd fled all those years ago. The town had truly turned against her, his brother, her friends, and the police included. His blood began to boil beneath his skin. They would get no answers from the law today, only a handwritten report shoved into a manila folder and crammed into a file cabinet. No one cared about his tools, himself included. What he did care about was Abby Warren. He was going to clear her name and restore her solid reputation if it was the last thing he did.

Chapter Seventeen

IT HAD BEEN a long day of unanswered questions. Neither she nor Chad knew how seriously the break-in had been taken. They both felt that the deputy had shown more compassion than the chief of police. Don Miller continued to harbor some harsh feelings toward her, even though he'd only been a deputy the summer the accident had occurred. Abby couldn't understand why he'd been so stringent all those years ago. That he still embraced the same hardheadedness now was baffling. To help relieve the tension, Chad had suggested a quiet dinner for two and she had readily agreed.

Smiling at the memory of his eagerness to impress, she stood in his kitchen and popped half of a red radish into her mouth. The salad was made and the foil wrapped packet of sliced potatoes and onions was ready. She gathered the remaining vegetables together and stored them in an empty drawer in his refrigerator. Turning toward the row of glass windows at the back of the house, she watched him. He was a grill master in motion as he slid two beef filets off the heat and onto the plate in his hand. His height and solid build were comforting. He'd had an attractive body in his youth but as a grown man, he was even more appealing. When he wrapped her in his arms, she felt cherished and protected. In a very short period of time, he'd caused her world to truly come alive. The sun glinting off the disheveled strands of his mahogany hair made her pulse race. He was smiling when he turned toward the house, unaware that she was staring at him. She met him at the glass door as she slid it open for him.

"Hey," he said, arching an eyebrow. "I hope you're hungry. These smell awesome."

She smiled back. "They look pretty good too."

Her teasing tone brought a smirk to his lips. He moved past her, set the black ceramic plate on the countertop, and turned back around with a mischievous gleam in his eyes. "Not as good as you do."

"Is that right?" she said, backing up one step, then another as he inched toward her. The look he gave her was a little unnerving and with a strangled giggle, she turned away from him and ran. Her long legs carried her along the glass wall and she circled around, leaving the large dining room table as an obstacle between them. Glaring at him with mock horror, Abby lowered her hands to rest on the wooden back of the chair in front of her. He growled and bolted, following her path along the glass wall. The pale yellow room swam before her as she squealed out loud and darted in the opposite direction, across the expanse of space between the dining and living rooms.

She could hear his laughter as he raced after her. In a quick burst, she angled her body to the left, and then to the right as she scampered toward the living room. She was leaving a good deal of space between them until Chad surprised her by diving over the back of the couch and catching an upper arm in his each of his hands. Before she could yelp, they tumbled forward landing in a heap on the hardwood floor. The good news was that he'd softened her landing by shielding her from the rock-hard surface of the floor with his body. The bad news was that she was now sprawled across him, tanktop to T-shirt, bare legs to jeans. Gulping in a quick breath of air, she could barely manage to speak out loud. "The steaks are getting cold," she stammered.

"What steaks?"

She slowly shook her head and worked hard to suppress the laughter that was bubbling up her throat. "You don't play fair."

He smiled and moved to cradle the smoothly curved cheeks of her backside with his palms.

She couldn't help but squirm beneath his touch. "Yeah, like I said."

"Abby," he said, the voice carried on a soft caress.

Her tongue darted between her lips as she stilled her body. She realized immediately that lifting her gaze to meet his was a huge mistake. His swam with a tenderness she was not accustomed to and she closed her eyes while her heart hammered within her chest. She'd experienced sexual encounters before but this was not one of those. This had all kinds of unfamiliar emotions attached to it. Her heart thrummed while her body shivered. She could feel the full outline of his frame while the heat and strength that was him engulfed her. He had a way of making her feel stronger, more resilient when she was with him. In fact, there was no other way to describe it than to say that being with him felt right. It was like a long lost part of her had at last found its way home.

"Abby," he said again, forcing her eyes open.

She focused on the firm angles of his face. He was much more handsome than her memories recalled. His compassion was endearing, transcending a decade. The desire he had for her forced her heart to pound a wild staccato of beats. "Shhh," she whispered, placing two fingers vertically over his lips to quiet any words that may follow. She needed that silence in order to pull her thoughts together.

His lips curled upward as he kissed them.

Her breath caught in her throat as she considered her current position. She knew she needed to voice her feelings aloud but couldn't force the words past her constricting throat. Her breaths came short and fast as his hand traveled slowly up her spine. She could feel his fingers move over the thin ribbed-cotton barrier of her tank-top. When he reached the base of her neck, those long fingers slid into her hair and she shivered again, barely registering her fingers becoming slack against his mouth. With the lightest of touches, he picked that moment to press the back of her neck forward, guiding her head down and bringing her mouth against his. She became lost in a web of incoherence as her body responded to his gentle caresses. His touch was almost too perfect to bear.

When he applied additional pressure against her mouth with his lips, her hands fisted within the neckline of his T-shirt and she pulled him to her. Her mouth opened wider and she felt a rush of heat as he breathed his breath into her. She heard him gasp and his hands moved over hers.

"Easy," he said as he carefully pried her fingers loose.

"Sorry," she said.

He slid his hands along her jawline and looked up into her face. The smile he graced her with was as equally sweet as it was sexy. It sent tremors of need spiraling through her. "Stay with me tonight," he said in a soft, coaxing voice.

In that moment Abby felt as though her lungs had entirely deflated her air supply. The desire for her to agree to his request was clearly reflected in his gaze. The words spilled from her mouth before she could stop them. "If I stay, I may never leave."

The smile he graced her with was one of the brightest she'd ever seen. "I can live with that," he said.

She laughed. "You say that now."

His answer was to roll her onto her back, scoop her into his arms, and carry her toward the staircase. "This is your only opportunity," he said.

"Opportunity for what?"

"To walk away."

"Why would I want to do that?" she asked, burying her head against his chest and looping her arms more tightly around him because she could swear he was taking the stairs two at a time. At the top, her quiet groan brought about an easy chuckle from him. She pressed her face against his shirt a little harder, not because she was anxious but to hide the smile that had completely overtaken her features. In this moment, she was certain she'd never been happier.

⸺ ◈ ⸺

A tense anticipation crept in as he viewed Abby's car parked in front of the house. Today, Mills Pond had been all aflutter with the news of the break-in. His chest puffed with invisible pride. It couldn't get any better. Chad had discovered the theft and gone directly to the chief of police. That he was spending the night apart from Abby said a lot. Had it been that easy? Had he really gotten his point across? He parked his truck in front of his house, yanked a purple canvas bag leftover from his high school days off the passenger seat and quickly clambered out into the darkness.

As quietly as possible, he slinked down the street, ducking behind the shadowed outline of trees and bushes as he moved. The Warren house was a big two-story Victorian that took up half the block. Before reaching the lighted street corner where it stood, he cut diagonally through a neighbor's yard and stealthily moved toward the Warren's lawn. It was after midnight and the house was dark. He tiptoed around the back, coming to a stop by the porch steps. From there he could see both Paul and Abby's vehicles in the driveway. Paul was still in the hospital which meant that both Joyce and Abby were home. He wasn't worried about Joyce's Sebring. It had been towed to the shop following her collision with the ditch and the repairs weren't finished yet. He hated to involve Joyce any more than he already had but she'd become collateral damage at this point. There was nothing he could do to protect her. It was Abby's fault.

Crouching down in front of the porch between two large overgrown bushes, he opened the canvas bag. Reaching inside, his hand slid over a metal container and a handful of shredded bed sheet remnants. Laying the pile of material on the ground, he removed the lid from the can of lighter fluid and doused the mound. Recapping the lid, he returned the half-empty canister to the backpack, grabbed a pair of blue latex gloves tucked in alongside and pulled them on. Picking up the pile of soaked sheet, he began placing swatches a couple of feet apart down the length of the porch. Once they were set, he walked back to the abandoned bag he'd left lying on the ground.

Tugging the gloves off, he bent to place them inside. Gripping the canvas in one hand, he reached into the front pocket of his jeans, producing a cheap plastic lighter. After taking a deep breath, he flicked the lever and an orange flame leapt up. He watched it dance in the darkness for a moment, a single flash of color gasping for air and life. If he couldn't force Abby to leave on her own, maybe this would finally convince her. It might even take her life. If so, his problem would cease to exist. With a malicious smile, he leaned forward, lighting the first couple of rags. The fire would find its way to the rest on its own. With a final glace at the licking golden flames that quickly began to grow, he turned and ran as if the devil himself was preparing to hitch a ride.

Chapter Eighteen

THE IMPATIENT RING of Chad's cell phone hovered about the edges of his slumber. Preferring the feel of Abby's soft warm body nestled against him, he ignored it and pulled her closer, burying his nose in the wave of thick dark hair that fanned out across her pillow. The scent of honeysuckle would forever more remind him of her. He smiled at the thought of forever. Their night together had been an incredible one and only solidified the fact that he would pursue her to the ends of the earth. Mills Pond was a nice place to settle, being that both of their families were here, but if it didn't work out, he would follow her wherever she wanted to go.

The phone chirped again, a loud protest in the quiet of the night, and he groaned. What time was it? Blinking his eyes as he turned his head, the red illuminated numbers on the clock barely registered one o'clock in the morning. Who would call at this hour? A sudden chill shot up his spine and his eyes snapped open. The lowlife stalker or thief or whoever it was would happily call at this hour. Chad cautiously rolled away from Abby and smacked his hand onto the empty bedside table. Aimlessly groping around the vacant surface for his phone, it rang again. His brain finally registered—jeans pocket on the floor—and he turned over, reaching for the pile of discarded clothing beside the bed. Sliding the ringing device out of the front pocket, he punched a button without checking the incoming phone number and connected to the caller. "Hello?" he said with a low grunt.

"Is Abby there?" It was a male voice on the other end.

"Who is this?" he demanded.

"Is Abby there?" the voice asked again, this time expressing a twinge of panic.

Chad's resting heartbeat spiked. "It's none of your business," he said.

"Chad," the voice said again.

A rush of dread burned through him as the voice finally registered. "Chase?" he asked.

"Yes. Is Abby there?"

"Why?" Chad demanded, impulsively becoming defensive.

"Because the Warren house is on fire and Abby's car is outside."

Chad's breath caught in his chest. "Abby's with me but Joyce is in the house."

"Not anymore."

"What does that mean?"

"She's standing in the yard screaming for Abby."

"Damn it," Chad said bolting upright. Running a hand through his hair, he continued. "Let her know that Abby and I are on our way."

"I will," Chase said.

As he disconnected, Abby stirred beside him, rolling onto her back and looking up at him with what he assumed was a questioning gaze. He couldn't tell for certain in the dark. "What's going on?" she asked. Her voice was soft and slightly slurred as she struggled to shrug off the effects of a deep, peaceful sleep.

Tossing the phone onto the top of his discarded jeans, he turned his head toward her. "We need to get dressed."

"Why?" she asked.

"Abby," he said in a slow, careful tone as he climbed out of bed, bending to pick up an abandoned pair of boxer shorts off the floor and hurriedly tugging them on. He then turned and flipped on the bedside lamp, blinking rapidly to shield his eyes from the immediate blaze of sufficient wattage radiating from the small bulb. "We need to go."

Chad couldn't help but stare as she sat straight up in his bed. The deep walnut stain of the lofty headboard helped to silhouette her slender shape as the sheet dropped to her hips. A quick intake of breath caught at the back of his throat as he gaped at the light suntan coating her arms and shoulders. His gaze greedily continued downward over the soft alabaster globes of her breasts and smooth stomach. Ah, what he would give at that moment to crawl back into bed and kiss her into oblivion. Instead, he pivoted on his heel away from her and stalked into the large master bathroom. Turning on the first faucet of the dual sinks, he cupped his hands and held them beneath the cold stream. When the pooling water began flowing over his fingers, he flung the puddle into his face. Abby appeared in the doorway at that moment. She must have read the urgency in his actions as her pale pink bra and panties were in place and she was tugging her navy blue tank-top over her head. "What's going on?" she asked again.

He grabbed a blue hand-towel hanging on the rod beside the sink and dried his face and neck. Tossing it onto the countertop, he turned toward her. Her face was tense, her eyes questioning when he met her gaze. "Your house is on fire."

"What?" she demanded.

"Get dressed," he said. "We've got to go."

She gasped. When she spoke, her voice was sharp with fear. "Mom."

He stepped past her and returned to his side of the bed and the discarded pile of clothing lying beside it. "She got out of the house okay but everyone is panicked because they can't find you."

She turned toward him, her brow creased with confusion. "Why would they think I was even in the house?" she asked.

With both arms anchored over his head and his T-shirt stretched between them, he stopped short of pulling it on. "Because your car is still parked in the driveway."

"Oh," she said quietly.

Shoving the shirt down his torso, he bent to snatch up a pair of khaki shorts lying beside his jeans and tossed them to her. "Baby, get dressed. We need to go."

Within seconds, they were both fully clad and running down the stairs toward the garage. Grabbing his wallet and keys off the kitchen counter as they hurried past, he followed her out the door. She took off to the right, circling the front while he ran to the driver's side on the left. She nearly bounced from the ground into the passenger seat as he connected his seatbelt and turned the key in the ignition. Her eyes were wide with dread when her gaze met his.

———◦《◉》◦———

Abby's fingers were stiff as she worked to snap her seatbelt into place, her racing heart feeling like it was wedged halfway up her windpipe. She was both tired and angry. Tired of the constant worry over what might possibly be waiting for her around the next corner and angry that it was happening at all. Returning to Mills Pond after all these years had been difficult enough. She'd expected to find some snobbery and possible ridicule, but the additional terror placed on her and her family was just plain unacceptable. One way or another, it had to end.

She placed one hand in front of her against the dashboard and the other, palm flat on the roof as Chad raced backward down the driveway. When the truck hit the gravel road, he stomped on the

— 160 —

break and turned the wheel with both hands in order to control the slide as the steel body careened toward the far ditch. The front end bowed, swinging the bed around behind them before coming to a complete stop facing in the direction of town. He gave her a sheepish look and slid his hand over her bare leg, momentarily distracting her from her thoughts. "Are you okay?" he asked.

Abby returned his unwavering gaze and gave a single nod of her head. "I'm furious," she said in a straightforward tone. "This craziness has to stop."

"I agree," he said, maneuvering his focus back to the road in front of them as he engaged the accelerator pedal and the truck lurched forward. "I just can't fathom why someone would go to the lengths they have without any concrete proof."

"Concrete proof of what?" Abby asked.

"That you can identify him."

She placed her smaller hand over the top of his larger one. "I've been thinking about that," she said. "I've done some research and found that the state statute of limitations for rape is five years. We're long past that. However, there is no statute for leaving the scene of hit-and-run accident. Throw in the fact that Holly died; the person found guilty of causing the accident would face jail time if convicted. In a small town like Mills Pond, a jail sentence could certainly crush someone's reputation, let alone forever alter the life of a family."

"True," Chad said.

"What if it's not about the rape or even Holly's death but protecting the good name of a family deeply rooted within the community?"

Chad looked at her, concern flashing in his gaze. "You realize that could be almost anyone in this town?"

"Someone who's been here for longer than a decade anyway."

Chad shook his head. "There haven't been a lot of transplants over the past ten years. More people have moved away than settled in. Given the current circumstances, I'm fairly certain the guilty party hasn't moved out of town."

"What about those new houses built out on the highway?"

"Believe it not, most of those are younger generations of long-established Mills Pond families. It's a lot of people who have lived here for more than a decade."

Abby blew out a quick breath as the glow from the town's street lights appeared in front of them. At the same moment, Chad let up on the accelerator as he sailed past the town limit sign going well over the speed restriction. Within a couple of minutes, he was pulling the truck to a stop a full block away from the house. The street was barricaded by a fire truck, two police cars, and a host of inquisitive bystanders making it impossible for them to get close. She had her hand on the door handle before the truck stopped moving and tried to jump out but the seatbelt snapped her back into place, spine first.

"Wait a minute," Chad said, throwing the gearshift into park. He reached over and pressed the button on the belt releasing her and somehow still making his way around to the front of the truck before she could. "It looks like the fire is under control."

He was right. Though the air was thick with the smell of burnt lumber and residual smoke, there was no sign of flickering flames or cinder glow. In that moment, the reality of the situation hit her. Someone had made an attempt to burn down the house with her and her mother still inside. A small cry flew out of her mouth and her chin began to tremble. Instead of offering comfort by drawing her into his embrace, Chad grabbed her hand and pulled her forward. More than a little stunned, she was content to let him guide her down the street at a full sprint.

Slowing down as they made their way to the front of the house, Chad pulled Abby along, working a path around the various vehicles. Circling a police cruiser and cutting in front of the fire truck, they located Deputy Nelson and Chief Miller. Both were tossing questions at Joyce Warren, each talking over the other in their excitement to get details. Dressed in a tightly cinched knee-length yellow robe and pink thong sandals, Joyce's gaze bounced from one man to the other in a dazed sort of way. The moment she spotted Abby, a sob burst into the air. Breaking the interrogation, she hurried toward her daughter. With outstretched arms, she gathered Abby to her and held on tightly. "You're okay," she said.

Chad watched the mother daughter reunion and felt his chest constrict with a pressure he hadn't realized was a factor. The lingering residue from the smoke burned his lungs and stung his eyes.

Abby gasped and her mother pulled back. "You're not hurt?" Joyce asked.

She shook her head. "No Mom, I'm fine."

Chad's attention settled fully upon Abby's pleasantly disheveled form. She was beautiful from the chaotic tangles currently ruling the top of her dark head to the very tips of her pale bare toes. He couldn't wait to be intimately introduced to each part that existed in between. Last night had been the beginning of something truly magical, something he planned to continue for a lifetime.

A quick tug jarred his current train of thought and regrettably, he turned his gaze toward the intruder. In this case, it happened to be his brother.

"You're here," Chase said candidly.

Chad stared at him for a long moment, angst warring with appreciation. He wasn't sure how to feel where Chase was concerned. "Thanks for the call," he finally uttered.

Chase's features grew taut. "What's going on?" he asked.

Chad nearly bit his tongue in half. "You tell me."

"Why would anyone want to set fire to the Warren house?" Chad rolled his eyes.

"You think I did this?" Chase demanded.

Chad lowered his voice and quietly hissed. "Someone did."

"Hey Chad, it's good to see you," Deputy Nelson said, cutting short any further discussion with Chase.

"How bad is it?" Chad asked.

"Thanks to the quick reflexes of the neighbors, the damage was kept mainly to the lattice work and porch railing. A couple of rocking chairs were destroyed but the house structure remains unscathed."

"How did it start?"

"We're fairly certain it was arson."

"How certain?" Chad asked, his gaze sweeping through the group gathered around them to locate Abby and her mother. They were talking with one of the volunteer fire fighters. With all the gear on, Chad couldn't confirm who it was. He was however, content that she was safe and he returned his focus to the current conversation.

"We're positive it was arson." Frank Wheeler, the fire chief volunteered as he stepped toward them, his gaze moving from one man to the next within the small group that had formed.

Chief Miller joined them. "How so?" he inquired.

"Chief," Frank said, "we found traces of lighter fluid on the ground near the porch. It appears that a cloth material soaked in the flammable liquid was used to ignite it."

"What would anyone have to gain by setting the house on fire?" Chief Miller asked, reiterating Chase's earlier question. Either Chase was really good at hiding his dark side or he was completely innocent. Chad hoped for the latter but it still didn't ease his anxiety over the situation.

"Are you asking me?" Frank said.

Don Miller nodded his head. "Yes," he said, his voice taking on a gruff quality.

Frank glared dubiously at the police chief for a moment before responding. "In my experience, albeit it isn't much, the only reason someone would resort to arson would be to eliminate incriminating evidence or to put an end to someone's life. Do you really think either of those is a viable motive in this situation?"

Chad watched the chief quickly move his gaze to the house and then toward the ground. The group around him stood there, impatiently waiting for an answer. Chad's gaze moved to Abby's. She and her mother had crowded into the circle opposite him. From the look on her face, they had overheard the tail end of the conversation and stood alongside them, waiting for an answer.

Chief Miller cleared his throat. "I'd like to think that neither of those is applicable."

Chad's head swung away from Abby's gaze as he confronted the police chief. "You've got to be joking," he said with disbelief resonating in his voice.

Frank Wheeler jumped in. "Chad's right," he said, "we can deny the facts until the cows come home but it isn't going to change the reality of the outcome. Someone deliberately set fire to the Warren's house tonight. The questions to be asked now are who and why?"

Don Miller sighed, an exhausted strangle of a sound, and turned his body away from the gathering. Before stepping away, he looked back over his shoulder, his gaze flicking from the fire chief to his deputy. "I'd like all the evidence on my desk first thing in the morning."

Gary Nelson nodded his head.

"We'll be sending some of our findings to the county crime lab but I'll make sure you have copies of everything," Frank Wheeler said.

"Do what you can," Chief Miller said and stalked hastily across the yard on his way to the car. It was evident he didn't like either choice. Given the information received from previous discussions, the time for denial was over. Chad knew the discovery had to be an eye-opener. He hoped now that Chief Miller would pay attention to what Abby had to say.

"Is it safe to go back inside?" Joyce asked.

Frank Wheeler turned his gaze toward her. "Yes, the house itself wasn't damaged. We've pulled the porch away from the structure just in case it reignites. You'll have to replace it and a couple of chairs," he said. "You can thank your neighbors. It was their quick deployment that kept the fire from raging out of control."

"I will continue to thank them for quite some time," Joyce said.

"We'll keep someone stationed outside for the remainder of the night to keep an eye on things," Gary Nelson said. "You were lucky Joyce, you could have lost everything."

"It's just a house," Joyce replied. "I'm very thankful that Paul and Abby weren't here."

Chad held back the urge to smile as he watched a pink flush rush across Abby's cheeks. He knew she was thinking about her absence tonight and the reasons behind it. Though he was certain he was the only one who noticed, it still gave him a quick rush of satisfaction.

"But you were," she said, her gaze directed solely at her mother's face.

"I'm okay, Abby," Joyce said.

"This time," Abby argued. "This continued maliciousness is not acceptable. It's got to stop."

As her words sunk in, Chad's jaw drew tight and his movements assertive as stalked across the circle to stand in front of them. "You are both staying with me tonight."

"It's not necessary. I'll have police surveillance," Joyce said.

"No mom," Abby said. "I don't want you to stay here alone."

"You can both stay," Joyce replied. A slight smirk slipped across her face as she moved her gaze between him and Abby.

"Joyce," he said quickly, distracting her from stating something that would make Abby even more uncomfortable, especially with a crowd gathered within eavesdropping distance. "We need to sit down and talk about this. Also, I'd like you to come with us to the police station first thing in the morning. Chief Miller has to have realized by now how serious this situation has become."

Joyce nodded her head. "All right," she said. "Are either of you up for a cup of coffee?"

Abby groaned softly and nodded her head.

"You two go on," Chad said, "I'll be right there."

Abby gave him a quick half smile and pulled her mother in the direction of the house. Content that they were out of harm's way for the moment, Chad turned back toward Chase, intending to finish the conversation they'd started earlier. Unfortunately, his brother had disappeared into the darkness of the night.

———◈———

He felt more than a little guilty as he watched the scene on the Warren's front lawn from across the street. It had been the perfect plan with one exception, well, maybe more than that. Her car had been parked in the driveway, but Abby hadn't been in the house after all. He'd had no foolproof way to confirm it. He also hadn't counted on the speedy efficiency of the neighbors. They had put out the blaze before the fire truck had time to arrive. And all the while, Joyce Warren had been standing in the front yard screaming out Abby's name.

The commotion had made the whole neighborhood come alive making it impossible to finish what he'd started. He'd heard snippets of their conversation and knew they'd discovered evidence of arson. Maybe he hadn't been as careful as he'd thought. The real question was whether or not he'd been careful enough. Leaving anything behind that might lead them to him would be detrimental. Anger seeped into his veins as he watched them. Joyce was an innocent bystander. Chad was fool. And then there was Abby; the way she continued to ignore him was forcing the edges of his sanity to haze a bit. She was the one tangible piece of the puzzle that could render his world a damaging blow. He had to do something to get rid of her because time was running out. He could feel it in his bones. He needed an efficient plan and he needed it fast.

Chapter Nineteen

AFTER SPENDING NEARLY three hours at the police station, Chad was no happier than he'd been the night before. They'd taken Abby's statement about the accident that happened years ago and added to it the events that had occurred since her return. Chief Miller remained skeptical. He even had Abby's original statement pulled from the basement archives so they could compare the two. With the exception of a few descriptive words, the statements were identical. He'd then blasted questions at her, one after another, trying to force a vehicle description other than that of a dark truck, an awkward personality encounter, or anything that might be helpful to their investigation.

He and Joyce were allowed to stay in the room with her as long as they kept quiet. Abby was a trooper though, letting them fire their questions at her without getting flustered. He was flustered enough for the both of them. She answered each one thoroughly and with as much detail as she could remember. She recreated the time leading up to the accident and then walked Don and Gary through the crash. She told them about Chase, his group of recruitments, and the continued harassment that had compelled her decision to leave town. She told them about the phone calls and the painted message left on her car. She and Joyce both gave an accounting of the false break-in at the lumberyard and being forced off the road on their return home. Chad shared the facts concerning his truck break-in, and they all discussed the fire. When strung together, it became a growing list of alarming factors that could not continue to be ignored.

Though round-the-clock surveillance was not something the small Mills Pond police department could offer, they did agree to increase their patrol for both the Warren house and the lumberyard. Chad wanted to move both women in with him for the time being, but both Joyce and Don Miller disagreed. They felt that being accessible might flush out the culprit more quickly. It meant that he would be staying at the house with them. At this juncture, he felt better equipped to protect the Warren women than the local police enforcement could. With that decided, Abby and Joyce headed to the hospital to visit Paul while he ran home to pack an overnight bag. After that, he was meeting Chase at Deadwood Dick's for a burger and a beer, not necessarily in that order, and then he would swing by Warren lumber to check in with Abby. It was difficult to let her out of his sight for even a moment but he didn't want to start off their relationship by smothering her to death.

⊸⊷⊱((◦))⊰⊶⊷

"I need to get out of here," Paul Warren said with an agitated sigh.

Abby occupied a chair beside his bed while her mother sat next to him on the mattress. The color had drained from his face as they'd relayed the activities of the past twelve hours. He was nearly as chalky colored as the room around them.

"Nonsense," Joyce said. "You'll come home when they release you and not a moment sooner."

As Paul blinked back the moisture forming in the corners of his eyes, he looked from Joyce to Abby and back to Joyce. "My girls need protection."

"Sweetheart, I know you want to be a hero here, but we're doing okay. The police are increasing their patrol and Chad is going to stay with us for the time being," Joyce said, lightly stroking his cheek with her fingertips.

"This isn't right." Paul insisted with a growl.

"No it isn't," Joyce said, nodding her head in agreement. "But the police are finally taking Abby seriously."

"Abigail, I am so very sorry that this has happened to you all over again."

Abby bit her lower lip before responding. "I know Dad," she said. "We'll have to pool our resources to figure out who's behind it. Once we know that, we can put a stop to it."

"What are the police doing besides beefing up security patrol?" he asked.

"Chad and I are meeting with Deputy Nelson later this afternoon to go through our high school yearbooks. We need to decipher which students still live in Mills Pond from those who've moved away. Chad is having lunch with Chase. We're hoping he might be willing to help as well."

"I still wouldn't rule him out of the equation," Joyce said.

Abby sighed. She felt the same way but for Chad's sake, she was allowing some leeway for the moment. "It was Chase who called last night to let us know the house was on fire."

"Exactly," Joyce said. "It's a little too suspicious if you ask me."

"What are you talking about?" Paul said, unable to keep the agitation from his voice.

"Chase called Chad to find out if Abby was there," Joyce said.

"When you were crazily screaming my name in the front yard in the middle of the night," Abby clarified. "At least you knew that I was safe."

Joyce blew out a frustrated breath making her bangs arc straight up in the air.

"You spent the night at Chad Austin's last night?" The way Paul annunciated the question terminated the bickering between Abby and her mother. The color was rushing back into her father's face like a pink sunrise warning sailors of an oncoming storm, making it appear as though smoke was about to come pouring out of his ears.

"Yes, Dad," Abby said. "I'm a grown woman and can make my own decisions."

Joyce smiled. "Abby's relationship with Chad has the town quite abuzz."

Abby gasped. "Mother!"

"Well, it's not something you can keep secret."

Abby groaned. "Especially in this town. I'm sure you had nothing to do with spreading the news."

Her mother's smile only grew larger, confirming Abby's accusation.

"The two of you are making my head spin," Paul said. "What else have I missed while being stuck in this sterile place?"

A nurse with short brunette hair and a fantastic smile waltzed into the room wearing bright polka dot scrubs, carrying a tray of food. "What, we're not exciting enough for you?" she asked.

"Not compared to what's going on outside of these walls," Paul said.

Nurse Nancy—Abby labeled her that for lack of a real name—deposited the tray onto the bedside table which had been abandoned to the end of the bed. "Rumor has it," she said with a smile, "that you're about to be released from these horrible prison walls."

"Not soon enough," her father groaned.

"I heard tomorrow is the day," Nurse Nancy said.

Joyce clapped her hands with excitement.

"We'll see," Paul said, sounding unconvinced.

"For a man that's about to be sprung, you don't sound very happy about it," Nurse Nancy said as she plucked a straw from its paper wrapper and thrust it into a clear glass of iced pale brown liquid.

From Abby's viewpoint, it looked quite unappetizing and she decided she'd rather not see what resided on the plate beneath the beige plastic cover. Jumping up from her chair, she startled both of her parents. "I'm going to head back to the house to grab a sandwich before going to the lumberyard."

"Okay," Joyce said. "I'll see you there in a little while."

Abby nodded her head and leaned down to hug her father. "It's good to see you, Dad," she said. "Now behave so they will let you out of here someday."

He chuckled but his arms gripped her more tightly. "Be careful," he said. "I don't want to lose you again."

Abby pulled back and gave him a solid smile. "You won't, Dad. I think this time, I'm here to stay."

"Chad Austin wouldn't have anything to do with that decision, would he?" he asked.

She only smiled in response, turned on her heel and hurriedly made her exit.

<hr />

Chase was sitting at a table near the back when Chad walked into the bar. With the pool tables in use, it was as quiet as any table could be. It was also out of range to be overheard. He was thankful for that. "Hey," he said, walking up to join his brother.

"Hey," Chase said and nodded toward the full beer sitting on the table across from him. "Sorry, I already started."

Chad's lips drew into a tight smile. "That's all right," he said as he yanked the stool out from beneath the table and straddled it with jean covered legs. Picking up the bottle of Bud Light, he took a big swig. Pulling it away from his mouth, he focused on Chase's face. "Where did you disappear to last night?"

"Home," Chase said. "I felt like I was in the way."

Chad lifted one eyebrow upward in question. "There were at least twenty people milling around. None of them were in the way."

"Fair enough," Chase said, "I didn't think I had anything to offer by being there."

"So you just left?"

"Yeah," Chase said defensively. "I ran into Karl, Darrin, and Donnie Burke on my way home. They were watching the chaos from across the street. Besides, you were kind of busy."

"Just a little," Chad said. "Did any of those guys act strange to you?"

"No," Chase said, his forehead scrunching up at the question. "What's going on?" he asked.

"Like I've been telling you, someone is trying to force Abby out of town. We're not sure who that is but after last night, the police are finally onboard."

Chase suddenly sat straight up on his bar stool. "You think it's me?"

"At times, yes, other times no."

Chase's gaze burrowed straight into Chad's. "It's not," he said calmly.

Chad swallowed the hard lump that had formed in his throat.

"I know I've been an ass where Abby is concerned, but I would never wish her any real harm. The fact that someone tried to burn her parent's house down with her and her mother in it is scary."

Chad took another chug of his beer. "Yes, it is."

"What can I do to help?" Chase asked.

Chad gave a heavy sigh that felt like half the world had just been lifted from his shoulders. The weight of the other half would be removed when they tracked down the person responsible for scaring Abby and her family. He put his hands behind his head and blew out a quick breath as he leaned back on the stool. Meeting Chase's gaze again, this time with both of them on common ground, he nodded his head. The waitress appeared then to take their lunch orders.

⸻ ⟪◉⟫ ⸻

Today was the day Abigail Warren would cease to be a problem. A police cruiser had remained parked in front of the Warren house until early that morning. It hadn't mattered, Chad had been there as well and that was something he had no desire to deal with. He'd kept watch from down the street, noting when the three of them had left that morning. He was certain the three-car caravan was headed to the police station. It was what he would do in their situation. After the arson attempt, he knew he was treading on thin ice. One slip up, even a slight one, could be catastrophic now.

He'd kept an eye on their vehicles. As suspected, they'd been parked in front of the city hall for most of the morning. When they finally dispersed, he'd watched Chad head south while Joyce and Abby had both gone north. Disguised in the form of his wife's nondescript Ford Escape, he followed the women at a distance, expecting them to travel in the direction of the lumberyard. Instead, they continued north through town. Once they reached the highway, both turned west. He suspected they were headed to the hospital to visit Paul Warren. That was a good turn of events for him. Their absence gave him time to prepare.

Tracing his path back through town, he maneuvered the car down the narrow city streets, driving a block further south than he needed, then west. The house directly behind the Warren's was owned by Edith Tinsley. She was an elderly widow, half-deaf and nearly blind. She had an empty carport behind her house which he carefully maneuvered the Escape into. Behind the carport was a thick line of lilac bushes which concealed one house from the other. He slipped through the bushes and as quickly as possible, made his way toward the Warren's back porch. Pulling a sharp pick from his back pocket, he jimmied the lock and quietly slithered inside. The only thing left to do now was to wait for Abby to come home.

Chapter Twenty

WITH BURGERS ORDERED and a couple more cold beers on the way, Chad looked across the table at his brother. "Why were you so horrible to Abby all those years ago?" he asked.

Chase sighed. "I was angry."

"Why?"

"Holly and I had been fighting for a couple of days at that point. She was feeling a little smothered and I refused to listen to her. When she told me she'd been accepted at a different college I blew up."

"Would that have been such a bad thing?"

Chase smiled sadly. "At the time it was devastating. We'd been dating for over two years and I couldn't imagine my life without her in it on a daily basis."

Chad pursed his lips together while the pool crowd erupted in merriment, hoots and hollers abounded along with high-fives and cursing.

"It wasn't just about different schools," Chase said, his voice distant as his mind wound through old memories. "She wanted a clean slate when school started."

"She wanted to break up?" Chad asked.

Chase slowly nodded his head.

"So you took Holly's decision out on Abby?"

"Not intentionally," Chase said. "She was just the easiest target."

"She didn't do anything wrong," Chad said in a voice gone soft with emotion.

Chase nodded his head again and silence ensued as he looked down at the tabletop in front of him.

Chad sat waiting patiently for some sort of admission of guilt from his brother. The waitress deposited another round of beers on the table just as the front door slammed open letting the bright daylight spill into the dark interior of the bar. Donnie Burke stalked in, took a look around, and made haste toward their table. "Have either of you seen Abby?" he asked.

"She went to the hospital with Joyce," Chad said, lifting the fresh bottle to take another cold drink.

Donnie shook his head. "Joyce is at the lumberyard. She claims that Abby left the hospital over an hour ago. She was going to stop by the house to grab lunch before coming in. Her car is at the house but she's not."

Chad was on his feet before the bottle hit the tabletop. "What do you mean she's not there?" he demanded.

"She has to be somewhere," Donnie said. His face had turned a darker color than the normal salmon in his angst. "I was hoping you would know."

Chad began moving toward the door at a quick gait. "I don't but I'm going to find her."

"Let me help," Chase said, jumping up to follow Chad.

Gus Anson strolled in before Chad reached the door. He was a half-foot shorter than Chad with dark brown hair set about a round face with chubby cheeks. He owned the farm implement company just down the highway. "Hey," he said, backing up a foot or so as the two came face to face. "Just the man I'm looking for."

"Hey, Gus," Chad greeted. "Why would you be looking for me?"

"Charlie Newton told me you had some tools taken from your truck."

"Yes, a couple of days ago."

"Well, I found a bag full of tools at the shop that no one is claiming. I thought they might belong to you. If you have time, maybe you could drop by and take a look?"

Chad had a searing pain rush through his chest as he met Chase's intent gaze. The last thing he wanted to worry about at the moment was his missing tools. "Okay," he said stumbling over the words. "I'll come by a little later to check them out."

Gus smiled at Chad, a toothy grin that would be appropriate in any other situation with the exception of a missing woman. The woman he had fallen madly in love with. Fighting to catch his breath he flung himself out the door and into the parking lot. Chase and Donnie were both on his heels. "Something about this feels wrong," he said as he turned around.

"You don't think Gus has anything to do with Abby missing, do you?" Chase asked.

"All I know is that we have to find her," Chad said. "We'll figure the rest out later."

"What do you want to do?" Chase asked.

"Hang on," Chad said, turning back around and sticking his head through the currently slamming door. "Gus?"

The older man stopped just short of the bar and his afternoon pick-me-up. "Yes?" he asked as he turned around.

"I'd like to look at those tools right now."

"Okay," he said with a sad smile. Reluctantly he turned away from his awaiting drink and followed Chad out of the bar.

When Chad was once again standing in the gravel parking lot of Deadwood Dick's, he glanced from Chase to Donnie. Gus Anson walked past the three of them on the way to his truck. "Donnie, would you go back to the lumberyard to see if Abby has shown up yet?"

"Joyce is supposed to call if she comes in," he said.

"Okay, would you run by the Warren house once more to check for her there? If she's not at the house, meet us at Anson Implements."

"Okay," he said with a quick nod as he trotted toward his car.

"Chase," Chad said, "you want to ride with me over to Anson's shop?"

"Let's go," Chase said, following Chad to the truck.

Within seconds seatbelts were in place and Chad was fishtailing through the gravel lot en route to the highway. "This just doesn't make sense," he said. "Why would Gus have my tools at his shop? And more importantly, where is Abby?"

Chase blew out a long breath of air. "I don't think its Gus you need to be worried about," he said in a rush.

Chad met his brother's stricken gaze from across the cab. "What are you talking about?"

"Do you remember the night I told you that I was playing poker with the guys?"

Chad moved his gaze back to the road but nodded his head in response. "Yes. That was the night Joyce and Abby were run off the road."

"Yeah," Chase said.

"What about it?" Chad demanded.

"There were eight of us playing that night."

"Okay. And?"

"We ran out of beer."

"What does that have to do with Abby?"

"Rudy Anson volunteered to go get more. It should have taken him fifteen minutes tops to run home and grab the case out of his refrigerator. He was gone for almost an hour," Chase said.

"Long enough for him to make an anonymous call to the police and follow them from the lumberyard."

Chase nodded his head. "He also drives a black Ford F150."

"Like yours," Chad said.

"Yes they're the same color, but mine's not nearly as souped-up as his."

Chad groaned. "Damn it."

"He could have easily hidden your tools in his dad's shop."

"I imagine that he was in the original group of harassers all those years ago?" Chad asked.

"He was my biggest ally."

"Chase," Chad said with a slow steady tone of voice. "If Rudy is the one trying to scare Abby, then he's also got to be responsible for causing the accident that killed Holly."

Chase closed his eyes and leaned his head back against the headrest. After a few quick breaths, he said, "then he's the one who attacked Holly as well."

"I'm sorry," Chad said as they continued barreling down the highway in companionable silence.

<hr />

Abby pulled her red Acura into the driveway noting the scorched pieces of lumber lying in a heap on the lawn. It was still hard to believe that someone had tried to burn the house down. The only positive was that the police were now involved. In fact, Gary Nelson crept by in his cruiser as she climbed out of the car.

He rolled down his window. "Hi Abby, is everything okay?" he asked.

Stuffing her keys into the front pocket of her jeans, she walked toward the police car. "Everything is fine," she said.

"How's your dad?"

She smiled. "He's feisty as ever. The nurse claims he might be released sometime tomorrow."

"That's great news."

Abby pointed her thumb over her shoulder. "He's still got a lot of physical therapy ahead of him but at least he can do that from the comfort of his own home."

"I would think that being home would be therapy all by itself."

Abby gave a quick laugh as she nodded her head. "You're probably right."

"Well, you have a good day, Abby. I'll check back a little later."

"Thanks," she said as she turned on her heel and headed for the back door.

She had a slight headache forming in the middle of her forehead. Hopefully a sandwich and Diet Coke would shut it down. The events of the past few days were definitely catching up with her. Staying up late the night before with her mother and Chad to talk over the increasing string of events had not helped either. When the first rays of light flirted with the curtains, she'd woken up to find Chad curled around her on the couch. Well, at least the part of him that fit on the couch. His legs from the knees down had been hanging off in a most uncomfortable looking way. Smiling at the memory, she turned the key in the lock and opened the door.

Brewtus met her with a squall of impatience.

"Hey boy," she said, reaching down to run her palm along the thick fur of his back. "Did I forget to feed you this morning?" She scooped him up with one arm and carried him further into her mother's Big Bird kitchen. Setting him down near the island sink, she turned her back and snatched a small can of cat food from the stack next to the breadbox. The darned cat let out another deep howl, the sound making the hair on her arms stand on end. "Dang it, Brewtus, you scared me half to death," she said, twirling her body around and slamming to a stop by a very large human chest.

The can flew out of her hand and crashed to the ground. The only sound in the room was that of the metal cylinder rolling across the cool tile floor. In the same moment that she met his menacing stare, Abby tried to recoil but his hands were already closing around her upper arms. "It's been a long time, Abigail," Rudy Anson said in a cold flat tone.

"I just saw you the other day," she said with a sudden perkiness to her voice that she was far from feeling. "At the bonfire."

He smiled a frightening smile. "So how is dear ole Chad?" he asked.

She fought to stay calm. "He's fine. I'm supposed to meet him for lunch in a few minutes."

"Is that right?"

"Yes," she said, holding her body up straight while his fingers dug into the flesh of her arms.

"Looks like you're going to be a little late."

She tilted her head back to look into his dark gaze. There was nothing in those eyes staring back at her to indicate that a human being existed behind them. Those eyes were cold and black and soulless. She knew then that her fate may very well follow that of her best friend. Swallowing the fear pushing upward from her chest, she nodded toward the phone on the wall. "Maybe I should call and let him know."

Rudy laughed a deep, guttural snort that shook her. "I don't think so."

"Then what is it you want? I can leave town if you'd like me to," she said.

He bent his head toward her, his dark hair falling over his forehead. "Too late," he whispered, moving close enough to bury his nose in her hair. He then took a deep breath. "I remember your smell," he said.

She gasped as he moved his lips over her cheekbone and trailed them down the line of her jaw. She put her hands against his chest. "Rudy?" she asked, her voice carrying on a quick breath of air.

"Hmmm," he said in return.

"It was an accident, wasn't it?"

"What was an accident?" he asked, pulling his mouth away from the skin of her neck to gaze down at her.

Abby swallowed a deep breath before responding. "Holly," she said.

He shook his head slowly back and forth with ominous glee glittering from his dark eyes. "No," he said. "It was supposed to be you."

Her confusion was clearly evident in her voice. "Me?" she asked.

"Yes. I dreamed about you for months. You know those wet dreams adolescent boys have? Do you have any idea what month after month after month of sex dreams can build up to?"

Abby shook her head. "No," she said.

"Insanity," he hissed. "I couldn't stand the wait any longer. And when I couldn't get you alone that night, I had to settle for a replacement."

"Holly?"

Rudy nodded his head. Abby witnessed the slow alteration of his facial features as they shifted from semi-attractive to evil. "All things said and done, it happened to be a very unlucky night for Holly Miles."

It took everything she had not to shudder in his grasp. "Why did you want me?" she asked.

His ominous smile was back, greedily eating up any recognizable facial features. "You were always the third wheel, the odd man out, if you know what I mean? I wanted you to fit in. I wanted you to be with me."

Abby shook her head. "I was just as much a part of that group as you were."

His voice purred. "Poor little Abigail Warren."

"What are you talking about?" she demanded, anger beginning to replace the fear that was racing through her.

He stared at her while his lips curled upward, peeling away from his teeth. "I always liked that spirited side of you. Does Chad enjoy it too? Are you as wild and willing with him as you are in my dreams?"

"Leave Chad out of this," she said, giving him a hard shove with her hands.

He took a step backward but pulled her with him and she found her feet suddenly dangling in the air before he dropped her to the floor. She landed on her back causing the air to rush out of her lungs. As she fought to breathe, he straddled her legs and pinned her arms over her head. He was about to attack her the same way he had Holly all those years ago. She swung her gaze around the room looking for some kind of weapon to use against him. As she was desperately searching, a large orange missile shot past her, claws primed for a fatal strike as Brewtus aimed for the whites of Rudy Anson's eyes.

The screams were horrible, both human and feline as Rudy fell backward while trying to dislodge the orange ball of fur from his face. There was blood dripping onto the floor. Abby rolled away from the fight and found her footing. Closing her fingers around the handle of the glass coffee carafe, she picked it up and swung it, solidly connecting with the back of Rudy Anson's head. His screams stopped as his body dropped to the cold tile floor. Brewtus realized at that moment his opponent had ceased movement and let go his hold. Those bright green eyes met Abby's. She was still standing there, poised to give a second blow with the plastic handle and broken glass shards that remained attached if Rudy Anson moved. When Brewtus gave her a look of dignified refinement, she lowered her arms and straightened her body. Satisfied with her reaction, he arched his back, stuck his tail straight into the air, and pranced out of the room leaving a trail of bloody paw prints in his wake.

Chapter Twenty-One

CHAD PULLED THE truck to a stop in front of Anson Implements, an old gas station and garage that had been converted into a shop and showroom for John Deere tractors. The grassy area between the street and parking lot was bursting with green and yellow tractors, large and small. In front of the dirty white building was a neat row of lawn mowers, riding to push. He owned one of each himself. He and Chase climbed out of the truck just as Gus Anson pulled up beside them.

"The tools are inside," he said as he hopped out of his truck and headed in the direction of the building.

Chad felt antsy as they followed behind. With Chase in the tail position they walked through the front door in single file. Gus moved through the open space of the glassed-in showroom, greeting employees and a couple of potential customers as he continued toward the back. The three of them entered a hallway with doors on either side. The four small offices were painted soft beige and housed a desk, computer screen, printer, and three chairs in each one. They must be the offices used by the salespeople when a big financing deal was going down. He'd never been in one himself. Of course, he'd never bought anything from Anson Implements that he'd needed to finance. The office at the end of the hall was large and personalized. It was painted the same soft beige with large framed pictures of John Deere tractors hanging on the walls. The first John Deere production tractor titled "Dain 1918" hung behind the large walnut desk, another built in the 1940's hung on the wall to his left, and one built in the 1990's hung on the wall to his right. Floor to ceiling shelves lined the walls on either side of the doorway and were filled with decades of John Deere memorabilia. Two brown leather chairs rested in front of the desk while a love seat and coffee table sat to his right. On top of the coffee table sat a fully stuffed black bag.

Gus Anson pointed to it. "Those are the tools that were found in the shop."

Chad walked over to the table with Chase following behind and hunkered down next to it. The bag was already unzipped so he reached inside and pulled out the cloth kit of marking knives and his hardwood bevel. He glanced at Chase who was standing next to him and grimaced. "Yes," he said, moving to a standing position, "these are my missing tools."

The older man shook his head. "I don't understand how they ended up in my shop," he said.

"Gus," Chad asked while keeping his voice low and steady, "do you think Rudy could have taken them?"

"Now wait just a minute," Gus said, his voice rising in octave with each word. "I'll not let you start accusing my son."

Chad put his hands up in front of his chest. "Gus, I'm not accusing, I'm just asking if it's possible."

Chase jumped into the conversation. "I've seen him a few times lately and he hasn't seemed quite himself."

Gus stroked his chin with his fingers. "He has been a bit preoccupied lately. I asked him about it because he's come into work late several times this past week and even missed an entire shift."

"What did he say?" Chad asked.

Gus shrugged his shoulders. "That he was having some difficulties at home. I've been there so I gave him some slack."

"My stolen tools ended up in your shop somehow. Do you think it's possible that he might be responsible for taking them?"

Gus stood there silently for a moment and then ran his hands across his face. "I suppose anything is possible," he said.

"Is he here?" Chase asked.

Gus shook his head. "He hasn't been here all day."

"Do you know where he is?" Chad asked, suddenly alarmed by Donnie's claim that Abby was missing.

"I have no idea where he is," Gus said.

Chad looked at Chase. "We have to find him. He may have Abby."

"Who's Abby?" Gus asked.

Chase responded as sensibly as possible. "Abby Warren is an old classmate of ours. We think that she may be in danger."

Gus chuckled at the comment. "Why would Rudy want to hurt anyone?"

"Gus," Chad said in a voice that immediately caught the man's attention. "We believe that he might have been involved in something ten years ago that is just now beginning to surface."

"What are you talking about?" Gus demanded.

Before Chad could answer the question, a loud roar erupted from somewhere in the building. The three of them abandoned the conversation and left the office at a sprint. Chase was in the lead while Gus brought up the tail end. The showroom was empty when they emerged from the hallway.

"To the right," Gus pointed as he kept running. Both Chad and Chase followed him to a door in the corner of the showroom which guided them into the shop where two salesmen and the two potential customers had circled around an agitated and bloody Rudy Anson.

Chad pulled up short and began to analyze the blood dripping down Rudy's hands and neck, pooling dark red spots onto his gray T-shirt. He had deep gouges on his face that were red and swollen and what looked like solid straight rows of torn flesh.

"What happened to you?" Gus shouted when he'd caught his breath and was able to view his son's appearance.

"I was attacked by a big freaking orange cat," he yelled. "When I find the damn thing, I'm going to kill it."

Chad's heartbeat spiked. Brewtus had attacked him. "Where is Abby?" he questioned.

Rudy's gaze moved from his father to Chad, then to Chase and back to Chad. "What you are doing here?" he demanded.

"Chad's stolen tools were found in the shop this morning," Gus said. "You didn't have anything to do with that, did you?"

Rudy snorted in reply.

"Rudy," Chad said again, "where is Abby?"

"I have no idea," he laughed. "All I wanted was for her to leave town."

"What are talking about?" Gus asked. "Who is this Abby?"

"Shut up, Dad," Rudy said, reaching behind him and pulling a revolver from the waistband of his jeans that had been concealed from view beneath his shirt.

"What are you doing?" Gus yelled.

Rudy aimed the gun directly at Gus's chest. "Shut up," he reiterated.

"Rudy, you don't have to do this," Chase said taking a step forward before Chad put an arm out to stop him.

Rudy shifted the gun, directing it now at Chase. "This is all Holly's fault," he said.

Chad blew out a breath while Chase put his hands in the air.

"Holly died a long time ago, Rudy," Chase said. "How can you blame her for this?"

Rudy blinked his eyes but remained silent.

Chase continued. "Holly died when the car she was riding in was forced off the road."

"Yeah, I'm sure that's what Abby's been telling you," Rudy said.

"Why would she lie about it?" Chase asked.

Rudy laughed again. "You were the one who ran Abby out of town the first time. Now she's back and dating your brother. Doesn't that piss you off?"

"It happened a long time ago. If Abby wants to come home and date Chad, I'd say that's between them."

"You were so convinced that Abby killed Holly. Why are you okay with her coming back now?" Rudy inquired.

Gus jumped into the conversation. "What are you—"

Rudy aimed the gun at the roof and fired. The sound was loud and intimidating at the same time. Gus jumped backward as Rudy once again aimed the gun at his father. "Shut up," he said. "I'm not going to tell you again." Keeping the gun trained on Gus, Rudy turned his gaze back toward Chase. "I'll tell you why," Rudy said. "You're willing to listen to anything Abby says, even her lies."

"What lies?" Chad asked.

Rudy gave a loud exhale of breath as he smiled. With the bloody mess of his face, it was both ugly and disturbing. "Of course you would listen to her," he said. "She's whispering sweet nothings to you in bed every night."

"She was terrified to come back here," Chad said. "She only did so because her family needed her. She's faced her demons. I think it's time you faced yours."

"You think I'm wrestling with demons?" Rudy asked.

"You certainly look like you have," Chad said.

Rudy laughed again, a harsh sound in the large open shop. "I had a good life until Abigail Warren came back."

"What does Abby have to do with you?" Chad asked. "Why scare and torment her? Why break into my truck and steal my tools?"

"She wouldn't leave," Rudy said. "She kept running to you and you encouraged her. Taking your tools was supposed to be a warning. Why didn't you just walk away?"

Chad felt like he'd taken a punch to the gut and he fought to keep his temper intact. "What did she ever do to you?"

The gun in Rudy's hand moved from Gus's chest to Chad's. "It was supposed to be Abby, not Holly," he said.

"What?" Chad exclaimed.

Rudy ground his teeth together. "I wanted Abby."

Chase groaned out loud. "You attacked Holly instead of Abby?"

"It wasn't personal," Rudy said.

"Wasn't personal?" Chase cried. "You raped my girlfriend and then ran both girls off the road."

Rudy shrugged his shoulders and the gun sagged slightly in his grip. "Like I said, it wasn't personal. I just wanted to keep them from telling anyone what I'd done."

At that moment, one of the men standing behind Rudy rushed forward. The gun lurched in his hand but he held fast to it. Chad moved forward to help but Chase grabbed his arm to hold him back. Chad tried to break free but Chase kept his hold as he stepped in front of his brother. They were standing face to face when the revolver went off.

It was as if the entire scene was happening in slow motion. Rudy's body recoiled as he was charged from behind. The gun swung up and then down as he fought the attack. The discharge was loud, the bullet fast. Chase was standing in front of him, keeping him from joining the fray. His brother's eyes suddenly grew large as his body thrust forward. Chad caught him as he fell. Lowering him to the cement floor, he felt a warm sticky substance at the back of

Chase's shoulder. When he pulled his hand away, it was covered in dark red blood. His brother's blood was on his hands. "Chase?" he hollered, "Chase, can you hear me?"

The room exploded with people. Three police officers rushed in and Rudy Anson was on the ground face first in a matter of seconds while the gun that had been in his hand skittered across the gray cement floor. Gus Anson had fallen to his knees as the fact that his son was being arrested for murder sunk in. Chase's face was pale as the shock of being shot penetrated his conscience.

Chad looked up and met Gary Nelson's gaze. "We need an ambulance," he shouted. "Chase has been shot."

As the deputy radioed for help, Chase reached up to grip his arm. "Chad?" he said.

"I'm here," Chad said, "hang in there. Help is on the way."

It was only a few seconds, maybe longer, when the gurney made its way into the room. The scene became blurry and swam before him as the attendants asked him to move. He slowly let loose of Chase's hand and stepped back to watch them prep his brother for transport. At that moment, two hands caught at the back of his shirt and he turned around to find Abby standing there. Her face was tearstained but she looked whole and healthy. "Oh, thank God," he said, grabbing her to him and wrapping her in his arms.

"What happened?" she asked.

"Rudy shot Chase."

"I'm so sorry," she said.

"It was an accident, but still."

Abby nodded her head.

"Did he hurt you?" he asked, running his hands over her face, her shoulders, everywhere he could reach.

"No," she said. "I was able to get away. Donnie was there when I ran outside and he took me to the police station. We were there when the call came in about a shot fired and we followed them here."

"But you're okay?" he asked, his fingers skimming her pale cheeks.

She pursed her lips and her eyelids blinked rapidly. "He broke into the house with every intention of hurting me. It's crazy but Brewtus saved me."

"I saw his handiwork," Chad smiled. "I never want to be on that cat's bad side."

"I had no idea I had an attack cat on my hands. I guess no one stands between me and his can of Fancy Feast."

Chad smiled a shaky smile. "I'm going to make sure Brewtus gets a key to the city."

Abby laughed softly and he gripped her tighter as they followed behind the rolling gurney carrying his injured brother away from the crime scene.

Chapter Twenty-Two

THE WAITING ROOM at the hospital was packed with family, friends, and law enforcement. While Deputy Nelson continued taking statements from those who had witnessed Rudy's unraveling, Chief Miller made a quick entrance and disappeared. People were having a hard time wrapping their heads around the fact that Rudy Anson had attacked and then caused the death of Holly Miles. Chase had been in shock when they put him in the ambulance. After assurances from Donnie Burke that he would deliver her to the lumberyard, Chad had jumped in the ambulance to accompany his brother to the hospital. A brief conversation had ensued once she'd reunited with her mother, and they'd hurriedly driven to the hospital as well.

While waiting for Chase to come out of surgery, Abby convinced Chad to visit her father. Walking toward the elevator that would take them up two floors, he stopped short, opening the stairwell door instead.

"Are you serious? Haven't we gotten enough exercise today?" She teased him.

"Come on," he said with a smile, pulling her through the door. They climbed the stairs to the landing halfway between the second and third floors when Chad stopped and turned her toward him. He hooked his index finger beneath her chin and lifted her face upward. "I thought I'd lost you today," he said, his voice husky with emotion as the words came out.

She reached up to thread her fingers through the hair at the base of his neck. "I'm right here," she said.

His mouth came down to meet hers; the kiss was soft, yet greedy. She groaned in response which motivated him further.

Sliding his hands to her hips, he easily lifted her body, took three steps and pinned her against the white cement wall. The kiss deepened and she wrapped her legs around him, her body thrumming to life against his. Her hands began tearing at his T-shirt, yanking the tucked hem free from the waistband of his jeans and running her fingers over the bare skin of his back. They were both alive. The stalker had been caught but not without casualties. As the reality of their day began sinking into her brain, a door below opened and footsteps ascended the stairwell.

"Damn," he said in a voice thick with need as he reluctantly set her back on her feet.

Fighting for breath, she gripped the front of his shirt with her fists while he shoved the back of it into the waistband of his jeans once again. Her heart was pounding in her chest, not from the physical intimacy they'd just shared but because words were floating up from within her chest. Words she now had no reason to hold back.

The footsteps drew closer and he grabbed her hand, ready to lead her up the flight of stairs in front of them.

She held back. "Chad," she said, her breath catching in her throat.

"What is it?" he asked, gazing down at her with a look flooded with sudden concern.

"I'm sorry," she said. "I never meant for any of this to happen."

He smiled a sad smile and traced her jaw with the pad of his thumb. "It's not your fault, Abby. You've done nothing wrong, not then and not now."

The steps on the stairs slowed and the door just below them opened. The person exited and the door shut loudly behind them.

He flashed a sexy smile. "Alone again."

She smiled back. "I love you," she said without thinking about it. The words just fell out of her mouth.

"What?" he said, his thumb catching beneath her chin as his liquid pecan gaze burned into hers. "I don't think I heard you."

She laughed. It was an easy tinkle that came from deep inside. "I love you, Chad Austin."

He smiled. It lit up his face and danced in his eyes. "Does that mean you'll marry me?"

"Marry you? We've only been dating a week!" she exclaimed.

"But I've loved you for more than a decade," he said. "That has to count for something."

She smiled and shook her head. "You're impossible. Let's go say hello to my dad."

They emerged from the stairwell on the fourth floor, all smiles and excitement. She led him down the hall and hand in hand, they walked through the doorway and into her father's room. When the full space opened to their view, her mother was sitting on the mattress beside her father while Police Chief Miller stood in front of them.

"There you are," her mother greeted.

Abby took a deep breath and tried to smile.

"Chief Miller was just explaining what happened," her father said. "Are the two of you okay?"

She looked at Chad and they nodded their heads simultaneously.

"Abby, Chad," Don Miller said as he looked in their direction,

"I owe both of you an apology. Especially you, Abby. I should have listened to you all those years ago."

"I'm just thankful that you finally did," she said.

"I can assure you that Rudy Anson will be prosecuted to the fullest extent that the law allows. How's Chase doing?"

"He's still in surgery," Chad said. "He'll be stiff and sore for a while but they claim he'll make a full recovery."

"Good" the Chief said. "I need to get back to the station but wanted you all to know that this should finally be over."

"Thank you, Don," Joyce said as he stepped past the younger pair on his way out of the room.

"You're welcome," he said before disappearing out the door.

Her father stuck out his hand. "It's good to see you, Chad."

Chad stepped forward thrusting his arm out for the handshake. "It's good to see you as well. Abby tells me that you'll be out of this place shortly."

"They're supposedly booting me out tomorrow."

"That's great news."

"Joyce tells me that you're dating my daughter," he said with a smile and a quick wink aimed toward her.

"Dad!" Abby groaned.

"I'm just hoping that you will influence her enough to stick around."

"I'm working on it, Sir," Chad said. "I've asked Abby to marry me."

Abby's eyes flew wide with the shock of his audacity while her cheeks grew rosy with the stain of embarrassment.

"What?" Joyce shrieked. "You're getting married?"

Abby let go of Chad's hand and dropped her face into both palms, shielding her expression from the group.

Chad confessed. "She hasn't given me an answer yet."

"And you think you're going to get one now?" she asked, dropping her hands back to her sides.

"Well, I suppose the proper thing to do would be to ask for your father's permission."

"You have it," Paul Warren said just a tad too quickly.

"Great! Then I'm taking my chances," Chad said, giving her a smile that was meant to wow the socks clean off her feet. In fact, she was looking down at her feet when the room erupted with laughter.

After their visit with Paul and Joyce Warren, he and Abby had gone back to wait with his family while Chase was in surgery. They'd only been sitting for a few minutes when a nurse came in. "I'm looking for Abby Warren," she announced.

"Right here," Chad said as he stood up and pulled Abby along with him.

"Could you come with me, please?"

They gave each other a startled look but followed the tall blonde surgical nurse down a brightly lit corridor to the left.

"Your brother is out of surgery and in recovery. However, he has become quite agitated about speaking with Abby. The surgeon thought it best that he do so before he tears out the stitches," the nurse said as she led them through a curtained ward that looked much like an emergency room. She stopped in front of a closed panel and pointed. "He's in here."

They stepped around the curtain to see Chase lying on a gurney. The heavy metal sides of the bed were locked in the upward position. His right shoulder was heavily bandaged and an intravenous line was affixed to the inside of his right wrist. He was also hooked up to a monitor that gave off an annoying beep every few seconds.

"Hey," Chad said, moving to the edge of the bed. "You're looking a little better than when they first brought you in here."

"Thanks," Chase croaked. It was evident that his throat was dry and even more likely, sore from the surgery. "I need to talk to Abby."

"I'm here," she said, maneuvering closer. Chad moved up behind her and rested his hands on her hips.

"I need to tell you something," Chase said.

She smiled. "It could have waited until you were settled in your room."

"No," Chase said. "I need to apologize to you."

"Chase, it's not necessary."

He grabbed her hand, sending the tube attached swinging. "Yes I do. I blamed you for losing Holly. What I couldn't admit was that I had probably already lost her before that night."

"I don't know if that's true," Abby said. "She was pretty upset about it."

"I do. We were headed to separate colleges and separate lives. She would have met someone else just like I did."

"Let her go, Chase," Abby said in a soft and soothing voice. "She would want you to."

"I have. I just need you to know that I'm sorry for everything."

Abby smiled. "Thank you," she said.

Chad was happy to hear his brother's words voiced out loud. Abby had earned them. "Get some sleep, I think you're going to need it," he said.

Chase nodded his head and they turned to leave the small curtained space. "Oh, one more thing," he said, "I'm okay with you and Abby dating."

Chad laughed. "Like you ever had a say in it, little brother."

"Are you okay with me marrying him?" Abby asked with a sly grin plastered across her face.

"What?" Chase groaned.

They both broke into laughter as he met her gaze. Sliding his palm against hers, he led her out of the small curtained space. Now that the mystery was solved, they could truly make plans for a long future together.

Chapter Twenty-Three

November 27ᵗʰ
Sixteen months later

THE TREES LINING town square were bare, their leaves having turned from their former fiery glory to littering the ground with a crunchy brown carpet. The day was cool and crisp with blue skies above. The parade had just dispersed and people wearing purple and white Panther gear were everywhere. Mills Pond abounded with excitement. As they walked through the park, Chad wound his fingers through Abby's and squeezed her hand. Her smile took his breath away. He couldn't believe that at the end of September they'd celebrated their first wedding anniversary.

Her dream had been to get married in the park's gazebo. He'd been more than happy to make that wish come true. Chase had been his best man and his sister-in-law Kate had been Abby's Matron of Honor. It was amazing how quickly Abby and Kate had gotten to be friends following the shooting. In fact, Chase being shot had been one of the best things to happen to them. Chad smiled. Chase may not think of it quite that way but he knew better. It had altered all of them, breathing new life and a change of priorities into their family.

"You two look happy," Joyce Warren said as she and Paul wandered up beside them. Paul had fully recovered from his injuries. He'd even overcome the remaining limp they suspected he might have to live with. It had taken a little time for Abby to accept the fact that Paul hadn't been disappointed in her. They'd had a tearful reunion at that point and he'd never seen a father more proud of his daughter. The day Paul had walked Abby down the aisle and tearfully given her away had been the most humbling experience of his life, especially when he was the lucky recipient.

"It's an awesome day and I'm with my beautiful wife," Chad said.

"Yes she is," Joyce smiled and put her hands on her daughter's rounded belly.

"Oh!" Abby gasped and grabbed her mother's hand. "Here," she said. "He's kicking."

"He?" Paul Warren asked.

Chad met Abby's gleaming gaze and smiled. "Yes," he said. "The doctor confirmed it yesterday. We're having a boy."

"A grandson?" Joyce asked. "I don't know what to do with little boys."

Abby laughed. "You raised a tomboy, Mom. You'll be just fine."

Paul was smiling when he pulled his gaze away from his daughter. "I went in this morning and got that shipment ordered for the Bitterman's," he said. "It should arrive Wednesday morning. Don't forget we leave Monday for our two-week Italian vacation."

Chad nodded his head. "I'll make sure it's delivered the same day."

"Thanks," Paul said.

Abby shook her head. "Dad, when are you going to accept the fact that we bought half the business which makes us partners now? I promise that you're in good hands."

Paul laughed. "One of these days we're moving to Arizona and you're getting the whole kit and caboodle."

"And we'll be happy to send you into retirement," Chad said.

"Who's retiring?" Chase asked as he, Kate, and four year old Megan waltzed up beside them.

Paul sighed. "No one yet."

"Good to know," Chase said with a smile.

Chad clapped his brother on the back. "Congratulations on the big win."

Joyce chimed in. "Absolutely, it's about time this town had another football championship to celebrate."

Chase smiled. "Thanks."

"It is time to celebrate," Abby said. "Is anyone hungry?"

"I could eat," Chase said.

Kate shook her head. "You're not the one eating for two."

Chad looked from face to face around the group. He'd been blessed with the love of his life, a wonderful new family, and a great life. He didn't know how it could get any better.

"Aunt Abby?" Megan asked as the group wandered in the direction of Macy's Cafe.

"Yes?" Abby replied.

"Has Delilah had her kittens yet?"

Oh yeah, how could he possibly forget to add Brewtus and Delilah to that growing list of happiness?

CPSIA information can be obtained at www.ICGtesting.com
Printed in the USA
BVOW071534041112

304574BV00002B/26/P